"You first this time," she said, and with a hand behind Ricky's head, Alice brought her mouth down and kissed her hard. She was instantly rewarded with that little noise she loved to hear, the noise only a woman can make — that slight intake of breath that's not quite a sob but more than a sigh. Alice heard it and deepened the kiss by gripping a handful of Ricky's hair and pulling her closer.

The kiss turned wild for a moment, and Alice heard that sound again when her tongue touched Ricky's. The hint of uncertainty and mere trace of resistance that had been there earlier was suddenly gone as Ricky melted into her arms. They kissed for a long time and then Alice rolled on top of her and straddled her body. She got her robe off and opened Ricky's already unbuttoned shirt the rest of the way. Their eyes met, and Alice leaned over to kiss her again before moving slowly down Ricky's body with only one thing in mind. You first this time.

HOT CHECK

by Peggy J. Herring

THE NAIAD PRESS, INC.
1997

Printed in the United States of America on acid-free paper
First Edition

Editor: Lisa Epson
Cover designer: Bonnie Liss (Phoenix Graphics)
Typesetter: Sandi Stancil

Library of Congress Cataloging-in-Publication Data

Herring, Peggy J., 1953 –
  Hot check / Peggy Herring.
     p.   cm.
  ISBN 1-56280-163-5 (alk. paper)
PS3558.E7548H68   1997
813′.54—dc21   96-39470
                                                            CIP

For Frankie

ACKNOWLEDGMENTS

I'd like to thank

Martha Prentiss, for sharing your HRCF dinner expertise: You made giving away large sums of money while wearing patent leather shoes sound like fun;

Lesley Salas, for your enthusiasm for this project: Your early comments helped tremendously;

Martha Cabrera, for a last-minute reading, the pep talk, and the two-versus-three-button discussion — it put a gleam in more than one Textile's eyes that day;

Frankie J. Jones, my partner in life as well as my first, second, and third reader, for your constant support and encouragement. I couldn't do it without you.

ABOUT THE AUTHOR

Peggy J. Herring is a native of South Texas. Along with writing, she enjoys traveling, camping, and reading. In addition to *Hot Check*, Peggy is the author of *Once More with Feeling* and *Love's Harvest*. Her next novel, *A Moment's Indiscretion*, is scheduled for release by Naiad Press in 1998.

PART ONE

Alice

Chapter One

Alice glanced over the invoices and knew immediately that things weren't going well. Business was still sagging, and the six months she'd spent restaffing and juggling employees hadn't helped any. She shuffled the papers on her desk and searched for last quarter's balance sheet before remembering that Gloria had also been looking for it. Alice opened her office door and called to her secretary.

"Any luck finding that file yet?"

Gloria reached under a stack of papers and pulled

out an inch-thick folder. "It mysteriously appeared about two minutes ago," she said with a perplexed squint. She handed it over and then nodded toward the other side of the room. "Mr. Langley's here to see you. He has a one o'clock appointment." Along with the folder, Gloria also slipped her a piece of paper.

Alice smiled at him and tucked the folder under her arm. "Mr. Langley from Hot Check," she said as she held her office door open. Motioning toward a chair in front of her desk, Alice looked at him more closely: mid-twenties, shiny black hair touching the bottom of his collar, a light blue cotton suit with a dark blue tie that he couldn't seem to keep his hands off of. *He's nervous*, she thought. *Good. I like that.*

"Please. Have a seat," she said. Alice had mixed feelings about this venture and even more about Joe Langley now that she'd seen him. They'd spoken briefly on the phone the day before, and Alice had to remind herself more than once that he'd been highly recommended by someone she respected.

"So," she said, scanning the slip of paper her secretary had given her. "Coney's Ice Cream Parlors had a sixty percent increase in sales once your jingle hit the radios. I need results like that."

He picked at imaginary lint on his trousers and smiled. "Tell me what you've got in mind and I can probably give you something in a few days."

"How much money are we talking?" Alice asked. Her advertising budget had no sense of humor.

"Two thousand," he said. "And you take care of

any studio costs." At her raised eyebrow he added, "Sixty percent increase in sales, remember?"

Alice nodded reluctantly. Results like that were hard to argue with.

"I assume you want a rock sound for the jingle," he said. "That's our specialty, but we can do just about anything."

"I want my sales up. I don't care how you do it." Alice tapped a pencil on the edge of her desk and leaned back in her chair to study him for a moment. "I understand your band is from Austin and your lead singer writes all of your material."

"Yes. That's right."

"I'd like to meet him before he starts writing. When would be a good time?"

Joe cleared his throat and sat up a little straighter in the chair. "We have a gig here at Muldoon's on Thursday."

"Thursday?" Alice pushed the button on her intercom. "Anything on my calendar for Thursday evening, Gloria?"

"A conference call at six," came the reply.

She looked over at Joe and said, "Your singer. What's his name?"

"Ricky Conrad. A she."

Alice set her pencil down and didn't attempt to hide her surprise. "Ricky Conrad's a woman?"

Joe Langley smiled again. "Yes. She certainly is."

"Hmm. Interesting." I haven't been paying attention, Alice thought. *I should've known that already.*

"We start playing at eight," he said, "but we'll be there setting up around six. You can talk to her then if you like."

"Thursday evening then," she said and stood up. "I'll give you my decision after I talk to her."

Alice was running late as she drove to Muldoon's Thursday night, and she could hear the thumping of a bass as soon as she got out of her car. Keeping her father's conference call short hadn't been an option. Sometimes she actually felt as though he *knew* she needed to be somewhere else before he started in on the endless questions. His conference calls were like pop quizzes, and Alice was never quite sure what type of grade she would get.

She paid the outrageous cover charge and allowed herself to be stamped on the back of the hand by a winking leprechaun. The place was packed, which surprised her. *It's Thursday night. Don't these people have to work tomorrow?*

While maneuvering through the horde of people, she watched the four-member band from the side of the dance floor. Alice ordered a gin and tonic and within moments was mesmerized by the young blonde on stage.

Dressed in 501s and a long-sleeve white shirt rolled up just below her elbows, Ricky Conrad tossed her shaggy hair away from her face to the beat of the music. She looked like a teenage version of Meg Ryan — thick blonde hair touching her shoulders, medium height, and a nice body that moved easily with the music. Her guitar was a light wood grain and her fingers slid up and down the neck as she sang.

But it was her voice that grabbed Alice's attention, a deep gravelly sound, like pebbles rattling in a plastic container. *Rod Stewart has a voice like that*, Alice thought after a moment. *And someone else ... some female singer ... what's her name? The one who did that song "Bettye Davis Eyes."*

Alice watched her with amazement. Ricky Conrad was both sensuous and dynamic, and she sent a burst of energy through the club simply by the way she grabbed the microphone. So this is the genius, Alice mused. She was surprised at how much she liked her already.

Joe Langley waved and motioned for Alice to sit at a table near the bandstand where beer bottles and empty glasses were scattered about. She worked her way through the crowd and sat down gratefully. As she continued to listen to and watch Ricky on the stage, Alice found herself caught up in the excitement of the music. She noticed the trickles of sweat that rolled down the sides of Ricky's face, making her skin glisten in the flashing lights. Alice liked the way she dried her eyes on the sleeve of her shirt between verses, all the while never missing a note on the guitar. That wonderful throaty voice gave Alice goose bumps several times. Alice was really beginning to look forward to meeting Ricky.

Alice watched as Joe tossed a towel across the

stage at the end of the first set. Ricky snatched it in midair and ran it briefly through her damp hair. She slipped into a black leather jacket that the bass player put around her shoulders. As Ricky turned to leave, Alice again caught herself studying Ricky's every move.

Joe came over to where Alice was sitting and pulled a chair away from the table and sat down. He folded his hairy arms across his chest. "She'll be here in a minute. She's changing clothes."

Alice squeezed the sliver of lime into another gin and tonic and stirred it briefly. "Tell me about her. How old is she?"

He leaned back and grinned. His tanned thin face and black hair made his teeth seem even whiter. "She's twenty-five. The most talented person I've ever known." Alice looked up just as the bass player came back with a beer for Joe and a glass of orange juice. He introduced himself as Stan Jordan.

Joe chugged the beer and ran his hand through his hair. "I can get the manager's office for you if you'd like to talk to her in private."

"No," Alice said, even though the thought of being alone with Ricky sounded appealing. "This is fine. Let's keep it simple."

A few minutes later Alice saw Ricky making her way toward them through the crowd. She'd changed into a pale lavender shirt with the top three buttons undone but still had the leather jacket draped around her shoulders. She stopped along the way and signed several autographs before making it to the table.

"This is Alice Collins," Joe said. He got up and

gave Ricky his chair. "Hopefully you'll be writing her jingle this week."

Ricky glanced at Alice and offered an engaging smile. "Hi," she said huskily. "I'm sorry about the wait, but I needed to change clothes."

Alice knew she was staring but couldn't stop herself. The goose bumps returned and scampered up and down her arms at the sound of that voice in ordinary conversation. Alice felt her head begin to swim when those powder-blue eyes met hers. Ricky held the look and seemed at ease, slowly taking her in completely as the gleams of mutual interest passed back and forth between them. *Christ, Collins. Get your hormones under control here.*

Alice lowered her eyes first and stirred her drink. "I like your music. I've heard some good things about you."

Their eyes met again and Ricky held the look. "Oh?" she said, and Alice felt certain that Ricky knew exactly what she was thinking.

Alice glanced away and forced herself to focus somewhere other than Ricky's chest where her ample breasts refused to be ignored. "So," Alice said. "How long has Hot Check been together?" *Good, Collins. Stick with generic chatter. Break the ice and get this over with before you make a drooling fool of yourself.*

"Seven years," Ricky said. "I've worked with Joe in other groups before." She pulled the jacket a little more snugly around her. "I've been doing this since I was twelve. In those days bands would break up in between our orthodontic appointments."

Alice cleared her throat and tried to relax,

9

secretly cursing the gin for not working yet. "Hot Check," she said. "I like the name of your band. Is there a story behind it?"

"That's the way they paid us for our first gig," Ricky said with a low chuckle.

That voice. I could sit here and listen to her talk all night.

Ricky fluffed the back of her damp hair. "Is there anything in particular you'd like this jingle to say? A certain sound you're looking for maybe? A phrase you're partial to? I can work it in. Lots of things rhyme with salad bar, you know."

Alice laughed and shrugged. "You're the expert. Surprise me." She toyed with an earring for a moment. A sudden desire to reach over and touch that thick, blonde hair brought a jolt to her whole being, but she pushed the thought away. Her attraction to Ricky wasn't a total surprise, but it certainly unsettled her. Ricky reminded Alice of a lover she once had in college. There was that same hint of rebellion that she found so intriguing and foreign. Being purely establishment, Alice envied those who weren't.

"Joe says you haven't made up your mind about us yet," Ricky said. "Are you considering someone else for the job?"

"Not anymore. It's yours."

Ricky smiled and gave a slight nod. "Good choice. I'll probably wrap it up for you this weekend." She took the straw out of her glass and set it on the table. "You seem a little young to be an executive."

"When your father owns the company, you can be as young as he likes," Alice said matter-of-factly.

Belittling her position in her father's company

10

was a habit Alice had gotten into in the beginning, more or less as a defense mechanism against the wisecracks from friends and colleagues. There'd been a time when the comments had bothered her immensely, but both she and her father were aware of Alice's contributions to the business. She was in training for the eventual takeover once he decided to retire. He wouldn't step down until he was sure she could handle it, and so far she was calling all the right shots. If Ricky Conrad's jingle could boost profits in the South Texas area, then Alice would look even more competent than her father already thought she was.

Ricky bit her lip and laughed. "So . . . how old are you?"

"Twenty-eight," Alice said.

"Are you married?"

Alice smiled and wondered briefly who exactly was being interviewed here. "No. You?"

Ricky shook her head. Alice again let her eyes drift to where Ricky's shirt began revealing a hint of cleavage. She forced her gaze away and sipped her drink, trying to rid herself of the image.

"Twenty-eight," Ricky said. "It would be interesting to know how much rock 'n' roll you listen to."

Alice was suddenly at a total loss for words. Ricky laughed again, the brusque sound coming from deep within her throat. She leaned closer and said, "It's okay. Music's a very personal thing."

"I like what I've heard here tonight."

Ricky took off her jacket and pushed up her shirtsleeves. "I guess that's a start. Is there anything else you'd like to know?"

That strange moment they'd shared earlier was back and made Alice very conscious of what she was doing, but scores of questions still remained, questions she wanted to ask, questions like, Is that marvelous hair of yours as soft as it looks? What does that voice sound like first thing in the morning? Are you feeling this attraction too or just fucking with my head?

Ricky smiled and pushed her glass away. She tousled the back of her shaggy hair and said, "I'll have your jingle ready in two days. I need to get back to work now. It was nice meeting you." She stood up, shook her head, and let her blonde mop fall into place. She went over to the stage and picked up her guitar, seeming not to give Alice another thought. Alice watched her exchange a few words with Joe before he came back to the table and pulled out a chair.

"Everything go okay?"

"Everything's fine," Alice said. "Make me some money, Mr. Langley."

He smiled and shook her hand. "I'll be in touch with you when she's finished with it."

As soon as he hopped back up on the stage, Ricky took the microphone and pulled it closer. "We're back," she said, her voice husky and demanding. The band came in with her immediately, and the dance floor began to fill up.

Alice finally dragged herself away from Muldoon's and went to her car and sat there for twenty minutes listening to the music spilling out into the parking lot. She wanted to go back inside and stay as long as they'd let her, but she decided against it and reluctantly drove home.

Chapter Two

The next day Alice wanted to meet with several of her restaurant managers individually. She'd seen three of them earlier that morning and was en route to a fourth restaurant near the northwest side of San Antonio. On the way over she found time to reflect on her visit to Muldoon's the night before. Those blue eyes and that shaggy mop of blonde hair kept creeping back into her thoughts like a slow, incessant fog. Ricky Conrad had definitely made an impression on her.

It had been quite a while since Alice had thought

about renewing that part of her life. A lover was a luxury she no longer could afford since relationships took so much time. *Why do it at all if you can't do it right?*

In college Alice had been considered more aloof and serious than anything else. She'd slept with several women by then but preferred staying focused on school instead of erotic bliss. She had goals to accomplish, and women occasionally made her lose track of what she really wanted.

After graduation Alice joined Collins Enterprises, and she set out to prove herself to her father and anyone else even remotely suspected of doubting her newly acquired skills. Associates who had been with the company for years didn't take easily to the boss's daughter coming in and sharing some of the same responsibilities that had taken them so long to achieve. As a result, any mistake Alice made came back to haunt her and didn't die out until she made a fresh one to take its place.

She had a rough time for a while, but her father assured her that it was all part of the learning process. He kept her in a constant state of training by transferring her to different departments within the company. She would learn the ins and outs of one division, run it for several months, and then find herself in a strange city with a whole new set of responsibilities. She lived the life of a gypsy for three years and had learned every aspect of Collins Enterprises within five. Her love life never completely suffered during this period, but Alice didn't pursue all opportunities that came knocking either. She had always chosen her lovers carefully. Getting naked with someone wasn't something she did often or easily. And with her demanding work schedule, who the hell had time anyway?

The parking lot of her northside restaurant was full when she arrived. This restaurant in particular, along with the one downtown on the Riverwalk, were the only two showing any type of a profit lately. Alice opened the door and found several customers waiting to be seated with no employee anywhere in sight. Alice moved through the crowd and spotted a few empty tables and a cluster of workers standing around in the back. One by one the employees seemed to be leaving and returning to work, each with a cocktail napkin in hand with something scribbled on it. As Alice got closer she saw Ricky Conrad at a table signing autographs. The restaurant manager hovered near her.

"Hi," Alice said with surprise in her voice. She took in Ricky's expensive soft leather boots, yellow silk shirt with a high collar, and caramel-colored leather pants that seemed to have been absolutely made for her. *Today she actually looks like a rock singer,* Alice noted.

"Hi," Ricky said. Her hair organized itself with no more than a shake of her head. "I thought I'd better visit one of these restaurants before I start writing about them."

Alice told the manager that she'd meet with him later. He excused himself and reluctantly left them alone. The other employees had already scattered and returned to work.

"May I join you?" Alice motioned toward one of three empty chairs at the table.

"Sure." Ricky closed her small notebook and moved a glass of orange juice out of the way.

"Did you drive in from Austin this morning?" Alice asked. "Or did you stay in town last night?"

"I drove back in. I've been here about twenty minutes. The traffic wasn't too bad."

Their eyes met, and Alice felt a slow, steady glow warming her whole body. *She feels it too,* she thought suddenly. The vibes between them were strong enough to crumble bricks.

"Last night at the club," Ricky said after a moment. "I . . . uh . . . enjoyed talking to you. Actually, I guess I'm a little nervous about all of this. I want your commercial to do well."

"That makes two of us," Alice said with a laugh. "Relax. I'm sure you'll do fine. So tell me. How often does your band play here in town?"

"Once a month usually. Sometimes more."

Alice fought the urge to ask for the band's schedule. She glanced at her watch and noticed that it was almost eleven-thirty. "Have you had lunch yet?"

"No," Ricky said.

"Would you like to see the restaurant downtown? We could have lunch there." Alice wanted to show off a little. Her restaurant on the Riverwalk was her number one moneymaker and a favorite with the tourists. This was also the excuse she was looking for to spend more time with Ricky.

Alice had the manager call ahead and reserve them a table, then offered to drive. She suggested they come back later for Ricky's car.

Outside in the parking lot Alice heard Ricky's low "Wow" as they reached the white Jaguar. "Jesus. What a great car," she said, gingerly touching the leather seats as soon as they were in traffic.

"I'm on the road a lot," Alice explained. "I like being comfortable."

"Hmm. And what else do you like?" Ricky asked.

The huskiness of her voice, as well as the suggestive question, sent another scampering of goose bumps along Alice's flesh. In the back of her mind she wondered what that voice would sound like in the heat of passion, but she tucked that particular thought away for another time.

Just as Alice attempted to formulate some sort of answer, a car zipped in front of them, causing her to slam on her brakes. Cars in all three lanes started honking. By the time traffic and nerves returned to normal, the mood had been broken and Alice had no idea what she'd been about to say. All she really knew right then was that she was looking forward to spending time alone with Ricky.

At the restaurant downtown they had the best table and started off talking about food and music. Ricky signed several autographs for the staff when she arrived. Her easy banter with them was almost as impressive as the number of people who knew who she was.

"This is nice," Ricky said a while later. She sipped her orange juice and seemed to enjoy watching the tourists cruise by in tour boats.

"Tell me more about your band," Alice said. "You're a lot more popular than I thought."

"Our new single's starting to take off. The radio stations in the area have been very good to us."

"There's more to this than radio, I'm sure," Alice

said. She noticed how men stared at Ricky, practically licking their chops. *She's got the whole restaurant's attention and doesn't even realize it.*

"The boys and I are going through an interesting period right now," Ricky said. "I've been thinking about letting everyone know I'm lesbian, but Joe wants me to wait for the right interview and let it happen that way."

Alice was a little surprised at Ricky's easy revelation about her sexual orientation. It made everything seem more intimate all of a sudden.

Their food arrived, and they waited until they were alone again before Ricky continued. "Then there's the question of coming out at all," she said. "It affects all four of us. Any kind of controversy could go either way for the band. We've been talking about it for a year already."

"Are you any closer to a decision?"

"Not really." Ricky's smile was tired and those blue eyes serious and piercing as she looked at her. "I've always had their support. We're more than four people who hang out and make music together. We're a family. I'd never do anything to hurt them. It's a big decision and they should be a part of it. We could very well crash and burn over this."

Alice sipped her tea and rearranged her salad with her fork. "In what way are they supportive?" Alice asked. "Are other band members gay?"

Ricky laughed. The husky sound made Alice's heart rate pick up a little.

"No," Ricky said. "They're three of the straightest guys you'll ever meet. I guess that's not really a compliment though, is it? We've taught each other a lot over the years." She smiled and tossed her head back, shaking hair out of her eyes. "They don't say dyke, fag, or queer anymore." They laughed together for a moment before Ricky continued. "And in turn I no longer nag them about the clothes they wear or express an opinion on the women they pick up. Those are the only real rules we have. And no drugs," she added. "We don't do drugs. We lost a good friend that way several years ago. We're all born-again squares now, and that's not something we want known, by the way."

"Why not? What's wrong with it?"

"Bad for our image."

"Really? You'd think parents would like that."

Ricky laughed again. "Parents probably *do*. That's the problem. Parents don't buy records. And what kid wants to listen to a group their parents like?"

Alice conceded the point. They finished lunch and talked about the jingle a little. Suddenly Alice asked, "Do you have to work tonight?" The thought of their time together being almost over was a little unsettling.

"Our first set kicks off at eight." Ricky drummed neatly trimmed nails on the edge of the table. "I don't suppose you'd be interested in going back to Austin with me this afternoon."

Alice looked at those questioning blue eyes and thought, *We're both moving in the same direction with this.* "Unfortunately," Alice said, "I've got a meeting later that I can't get out of."

Ricky sat back in her chair, the disappointment evident in her expression, but Alice had already made up her mind to drive to Austin later after her meeting was over. At some point before Hot Check finished their last set tonight, Alice hoped to be there listening to them. And that was as far ahead as she cared to think.

"Has being here today helped any?" Alice asked as they got ready to leave. "Are the creative juices flowing now that you've seen a few restaurants?"

Ricky slowly searched Alice's face before she said, "Oh, yes. The juices are definitely flowing."

Alice let that remark stand without comment since she had juices of her own to deal with.

They left the restaurant and drove back across town where Ricky's car was parked. In order to get her feelings under control, Alice focused on the familiar and asked more questions about the band and how long they'd been involved in advertising. Hot Check's credentials were impressive, and Alice felt better about her decision to hire them the more she listened to Ricky talk. Once she pulled into the parking lot, Alice could think of no other viable excuse to prolong Ricky's stay. She asked where Hot Check was playing that night.

"Friday nights are big," Ricky said. "We'll be at Sugar Daddy's on Sixth Street in Austin." She leaned her head against the seat and turned to look at her.

"I'll be there," Alice said.

Ricky laughed, her low husky voice sounding so sensual. She opened the door and met Alice's gaze directly. "If only you were serious."

Surprised, Alice asked, "What makes you think I'm not?"

Ricky's expression had a touch of sadness as she whispered, "Because I want it too much." She got out of the car and held the door open. "Joe will give you a call when the jingle's finished. I had a great time today. Thanks for lunch." She got into her car and drove away, never once looking back.

The rest of the day was one crisis after another. A water main had broken in front of one restaurant, resulting in no water for three hours during the dinner rush, and a bad storm had swept through Harlingen in the valley, causing downed power lines and roof damage to her restaurant there. Food would be spoiling shortly, and Alice's manager wasn't handling the stress well.

Alice threw some clothes in a suitcase and instead of heading out for Austin to see Ricky again, she found herself on the way to the valley having to work.

"It's fate," she mumbled, tossing her suitcase in the car. She turned her air conditioner up another notch and tried to soothe her frustration and disappointment with a blast of cool air.

Two days later, on Alice's first day back from the valley, Joe Langley showed up with a demo tape of Ricky's jingle. He set the boom box on Alice's desk and pushed a button to start the music.

Alice heard a consistent, steady drumbeat before the guitars and bass came in. The music was laid back but snappy — a sound usually referred to as "swamp rock," Joe informed her. He turned the volume up, and Ricky's voice filled the room. When

21

the music faded out, Joe pushed the rewind button and took a neatly folded sheet of paper from his coat pocket and handed it to her.

"Read the lyrics and listen this time." He pushed the play button again.

Alice tried studying the words, but the voice from the cassette player kept haunting her. A clear vision of those blue eyes and that blonde shock of hair was firmly engraved in her brain. She'd been staying awake at night thinking about Ricky and getting up every morning wondering if she'd ever see her again. The voice and the music grabbed her attention again, and all Alice could do now was listen and unconsciously tap her foot. Everything about the jingle was perfect. Instinct told her that this was one of those commercials that would be hummed on playgrounds, at bridge parties, in boats, on freeways, everywhere.

"I like it," Alice heard Gloria say from the door.

Who wouldn't like it? Alice thought. It was perfect.

"Well?" Joe said. "How'd we do? Is it okay?"

"It's wonderful," Alice said. "It's much better than I expected."

Joe let out a deep breath and laughed. "Ricky's amazing, isn't she?" He took another tape out of his coat pocket and popped it in the cassette player. "This is your commercial with the voice-overs and everything else added. We finished it this morning."

Alice listened to it twice more before writing him a check. Joe agreed to take care of distribution and all arrangements for buying airtime on the radio. They signed all the paperwork, shook hands, and he was gone.

"Are you okay?" Gloria asked. She hadn't moved from her position by Alice's door.

"I don't have her phone number," Alice said. She couldn't believe that she'd let him leave without getting it.

"Have you tried directory assistance?"

"I'm sure it's unlisted," Alice said, now truly depressed. "She's got quite a following already." She picked up the demo tape Joe had left for her and looked at it closely before setting it back down again. "Check directory assistance for me anyway," Alice said. "Just in case." She snatched the tape up again and then tossed it back on her desk. Her schedule over the next few weeks was unbelievable, and a quick trip to Austin to see Ricky wasn't possible.

Sometimes fate really sucks. Glancing at her watch, she remembered that she had to catch a plane to Dallas in an hour. *It really, really sucks.*

Chapter Three

Alice continued thinking about Ricky but finally gave up the idea of seeing her again. Despite the casual flirting and their obvious attraction for each other, their relationship had consisted of business, and now their business dealings were over. *It's finished, it was fun, now I need to get on with my life.*

There were more trips to Dallas and the official end of tourist season to deal with. Alice stayed busy and preferred it that way. Toward the end of September, she was invited to a small party at a friend's house where they were getting together for an HBO special featuring a lesbian comedienne.

"You have to come," Dora said on the phone. "It's a bonding thing. We all sit around in our Birkenstocks and talk about whoever's not there. It's a lotta fun. You'll love it."

"Watching the hair on our legs grow. I can hardly wait," Alice said dryly.

"It's been months since we've seen you," Dora said. "Come on. Trust me. It'll be fun!"

Dora and her lover Marge had been together for ten years. They were several years older than Alice, but the three of them had been friends for what seemed like forever. Dora was a private investigator, and Alice used her occasionally when she had problems with employees or when she needed something sensitive handled. Marge's three teenage daughters lived with them and were ad-libbing puberty fairly well. Along with Alice, two other friends had been invited for the festivities — Christine Marlow, a real estate agent, and Lola Colby, San Antonio's lesbian attorney-at-large. Alice was the only one among them who'd never heard of the comedienne everyone was so excited about.

After a quick dinner they endured Christine's spending a good part of an hour going on and on about a flight attendant she'd been dating recently. "The things a girl has to do for those frequent-flyer miles," she said, rolling her eyes.

"Then you've probably got enough to fly to the moon and back by now," Alice noted.

Christine was a tall, elegant woman in her early thirties, with tiny traces of dark roots beginning to show in her honey-colored hair. She was aware of her attractiveness and enjoyed flaunting her femininity. She stuck her tongue out at Alice in an undignified way.

"Has anyone heard about that new use for Preparation H?" Lola asked. "I heard it on the radio yesterday. People are putting it under their eyes to take away puffiness and wrinkles."

"I could use a whole case on this neck of mine," Dora said as she pointed to her throat. "Check out these wrinkles."

Alice patted her on the arm and whispered, "Save your money. It probably only works if you're an asshole."

Lola pulled the tab on a Diet Coke and then ran a finger over her left cheekbone. "I tried it this morning and I swear to God I think it's working already."

Alice raised an eyebrow and caught Dora's amused look. "Need I say more?" Alice whispered.

They snacked on popcorn and drank wine, always keeping an eye on the clock so they wouldn't miss the program. A while later over turtle cheesecake and coffee someone commented about hearing Alice's new commercial on the radio.

"I've even heard people at work talking about it," Marge said.

"Really?" Alice smiled. Her father had called earlier in the week to say how much he liked it too. Profits were already higher than Alice ever imagined they'd be, and the commercial had only been playing for two weeks.

Lola pulled something from her purse and waved

it through the air. "I've got tickets for the Human Rights Campaign Fund dinner to sell. It's next week. Get 'em now and we can all sit together."

Dora groaned when she heard the price of the tickets. "A hundred bucks for fish sticks, peas, and cranberry compote? I don't even know what a compote is, for cryin' out loud."

"It's that stuff you keep in a pile and use for fertilizer or something," Christine said.

"That's *compost*," Alice said, "and I don't think we'll be having any of that."

"When have we ever served you fish sticks?" Lola demanded. "The food's always great, and it's for a good cause, so quit your bitchin'." She snapped her fingers rudely and pointed at each of them. "We're all going again this year. Remember how much fun we had last time? I expect a fat check from each of you before we leave here tonight."

The following Friday evening Alice picked up Dora and Marge and was delighted by the transformation of those two in formal attire. The first two years that Alice had purchased tickets for the black-tie HRCF dinner she hadn't gone, but the last two times she had actually attended and enjoyed herself.

"You look great!" Dora said as she got in the front seat of the Jaguar.

Alice's salmon-colored dress had a slit up the side, exposing more leg than she was used to. She had decided to go all out this year. The usual cocktail gowns she wore at business affairs with her parents in Dallas were a bit more conservative than she felt like being tonight.

"You look pretty good yourself," Alice said, meaning every word of it. Dora's black dress fit her perfectly, and her short gray hair had a touch of curl in it. Marge wore a long white dress with matching heels and had a corsage neatly pinned on.

"We look like a bunch of dykes in dresses, but what the hell," Dora said. "Let's go. I've been looking forward to trying that compote stuff all day."

They found a parking place and were joined by Lola and Christine outside the ballroom. Everyone looked gorgeous in their high formal evening wear, and the entire floor of the hotel seemed to be caught up in the glamour of it all.

The ballroom had scores of large round tables covered with white linen and decorative, colorful floral centerpieces. A stage was in the middle and a bar on the other side of the room. More people were arriving as Christine led the way to the bar and purchased the first round of drinks.

"These shoes are killing me," Dora said.

Alice checked out Dora's black heels and laughed when Dora leaned over and said, "There's something masochistic about wearing clothes that hurt."

"Take them off when we sit down," Alice suggested.

"Good idea. Alice is ready to sit down," Dora announced to the group. "Where's our table?"

"We haven't mingled yet," Christine grumbled.

"Dora, honey," Marge said, "I think we're the oldest two people here. What's going on?"

"You're not old," Alice said.

"Hey, we're pushin' forty-nine," Dora reminded her. "That's a big number. And right now my feet feel ancient."

"Forty-nine's not old," Alice said. "It's only seven in dog years."

Dora let out a war whoop and gave her a hug. They spotted friends they hadn't seen since last year's dinner and waved them over. The music had started, and the room was beginning to fill up nicely.

"Oh, my," Lola sighed a few minutes later — her mouth slightly agape. "White tux by the program table. I'd give anything for some of that."

"Mmm," Christine said. "Not bad at all. Maybe she's a door prize or something."

Lola made a little grrr sound that sent laughter down the drink line. She leaned closer and said, "If they're selling raffle tickets for her, I'll buy them all."

Alice looked over at the program table and caught her breath as she saw Ricky Conrad standing there in a white tuxedo.

"Isn't that the mayor she's talking to?" Lola said, squinting across the room.

Alice bought another drink and tipped the bartender generously. Before tonight if someone had asked her to try to picture Meg Ryan in a white tuxedo, she couldn't have done it, but seeing Ricky Conrad in one made it a very pleasant picture indeed.

Alice picked up her Diet Coke and the glass of orange juice she'd just purchased and made her way around the tables. She wanted to apologize to Ricky for not showing up in Austin as promised a few

29

weeks ago. If Ricky was annoyed about getting stood up, then Alice hoped to have things smoothed over before the evening came to an end.

She noticed Ricky's smile right away, and Alice immediately felt better. The lingering eye contact was just as sensual and thrilling now as it had been the other two times they'd seen each other. Alice could visualize her friends watching her, mouths open, and eyebrows arched in astonishment. The mayor and his entourage were meeting another group of arrivals just as Alice reached her.

"Working the crowd, Ms. Collins?" Ricky asked. Her voice was low and throaty, the smile friendly and warm.

"It's a little early for that yet." She handed Ricky the drink and liked the surprise that flickered across her face. "Orange juice with extra ice, right?"

Ricky laughed softly. "I can't believe you remember that."

You'd be amazed what I remember about you. They were looking at each other again, and Alice felt a rush of longing and the tumble of excitement. She didn't hear Basia's voice as the DJ changed music, nor did she notice the crowd pressing in around them as more people began to arrive. The only thing Alice was aware of was Ricky and those incredible blue eyes.

"I'm sorry I never made it to Austin," Alice said. "Something came up at the last minute."

Ricky sipped her orange juice and said, "My loss." She smiled and asked Alice where she was sitting.

"Over there by the bar. What about you? Are you here alone?"

"An ad agency here in San Antonio wants me to

work for them. I agreed to attend this event and listen to their offer if they'd make a nice donation."

A stocky, bearded man in a pinstriped suit elbowed his way in front of her to shake Ricky's hand. "Miko Sarducci from KZIT radio," he said. "We need to get you on the show again and talk about your new album."

Ricky pulled a business card from inside her coat and gave it to him. "Get in touch with Joe Langley. He'll set something up."

Alice peeked around him and waved. "You're busy. We'll talk later."

"Don't go yet," Ricky said, but someone else stuck a program and a pen in front of her for an autograph.

Alice waved again and started back toward the table where her friends were still standing. She would make it a point to ask Ricky to dance later. *Seeing her here is too big of a coincidence, Collins. You need to make the most of this.*

Dora and Marge were grinning outrageously when Alice returned. Christine and Lola began asking questions so fast that Alice couldn't understand a word either of them was saying.

"You actually *know* her?"

"Introduce us, you stingy thing!"

"Is she really gay or just here to make a few points as the mayor is?"

"Christ, she's gorgeous!"

"Is she wearing sneakers with that tux, Alice?"

"Who's she sitting with? We've got room at our table!"

Alice looked back over her shoulder at Ricky and the people surrounding her. Ricky looked up at the same time and there was more of that heart-stopping eye contact. Alice held her drink in both hands and watched as Ricky said something to the group she was with and scanned the crowd again.

"Holy shit," Christine said. "She's coming this way."

"And she's not wearing sneakers," Lola cooed. "Those are white boots. That's it. Next year we're all wearing tuxedos."

Alice ignored them and went to meet Ricky halfway. She was nervous and excited. The evening was taking on a whole new meaning. Much more than eye contact and suggestive conversation was happening between them now.

"Hi," Ricky said, her husky voice still a pleasant surprise. "I . . . uh . . . was wondering if you'd like to go for coffee or something later. After all this is over."

"Sure," Alice said. Her heart was thumping along steadily. "There's a Denny's across the street," she suggested. *Go for broke, Collins. You already know what you want.* Alice lowered her voice and said, "Or there's always room service."

They were looking at each other again, and Alice could see Ricky's slow smile as she tossed her hair out of her eyes.

"If only you were serious," she said.

"I've never been more serious in my life," Alice said. She reached up and touched Ricky's hair, gently sweeping a lock away from her forehead. She was suddenly unable to keep her hands off of her. Ricky closed her eyes and visibly trembled as one of Alice's fingers trailed a slow, steady line down her cheek. "I've never wanted anything the way I want you,"

Alice said, desire gripping her whole being. "Let's forget about room service. My place is a much better idea. We can leave right now if you like."

Ricky nodded. "Let's go. I'll meet you out front."

Alice returned to her friends and quickly made arrangements to have someone take Dora and Marge home later. She had to endure several probing questions before they'd let her leave.

"Where do you think you're going?" Christine demanded. "It hasn't even *started* yet."

Alice collected her purse and HRCF program. "Something's come up."

"A little blonde something?" Christine asked. "You're actually *leaving* with her?"

Alice chuckled and gave them all hugs. Christine was still sniping at her when she left.

Outside the ballroom Ricky was talking to the disk jockey again, but she politely got rid of him the moment she saw Alice.

"You're here," Ricky said. "I keep wondering if you'll change your mind again."

"Not a chance," Alice said as she led the way through the lobby. "You're underestimating the effect that tuxedo is having on me."

Outside in the muggy September air, the nightlife of San Antonio was a buzz of activity. They were swept away with tourists on the sidewalk and found themselves dodging traffic with everyone else.

"I'm parked right over here," Alice said. She could see what a truly unique and desirable woman Ricky was as total strangers kept stealing glances at them. A new surge of excitement rushed through Alice's body when they reached the car.

Neither of them spoke until they were both safe behind the Jaguar's tinted windows. Ricky leaned over to kiss her and Alice felt the tumbling in her stomach begin. She let herself be pulled into Ricky's arms, and Alice knew that she had waited her whole life for this moment. The usual calm, detached nature that she liked to associate with herself was a thing of the past. Ricky Conrad had reawakened something in her that hadn't been there in a long time and had possibly never been there at all before this.

Ricky's mouth was soft and hungry, her tongue searching and bold, causing a fire to sweep through Alice with such yearning intensity that Alice could have come right there. The kiss continued, slow and consuming, and Alice filled her hands with Ricky's hair and heard herself make a pleading, murmuring noise when Ricky began exploring her throat.

"Not here," Ricky said. Her husky whisper graced Alice's ear and sent a zap of tingling energy down her body again. "Drive me to my car. I'll follow you to your place."

Alice reluctantly agreed but kissed her again anyway. The heat between her legs was turning into a slow, steady ache as she eventually pulled away from her and started the car.

Chapter Four

Once they arrived at her apartment, Alice took Ricky's hand and led her into the living room. Alice had imagined this moment a hundred times since their lunch together several weeks ago, but she had somehow forgotten how strong the attraction had been. Ricky leaned over and kissed her with a possessiveness that quickly renewed the fire between them. Ricky started a trail of kisses just below Alice's ear and moved down to her throat, causing the fluttering in Alice's stomach to begin all over again.

Alice put her hand behind Ricky's head and wove

her fingers through her silky hair. Ricky's mouth became demanding again, like that of a seasoned lover, and her tongue danced in Alice's mouth, making Alice's knees suddenly weak.

"Let's go upstairs," Alice said breathlessly, leading the way to her bedroom where another rush of deep, heated kisses began. Alice wanted to touch her and hear that husky voice. They broke away from one another long enough for Alice to slip the white jacket off Ricky's shoulders and slowly tug on her shirt.

Alice nuzzled Ricky's neck and caught a brief hint of perfume as she fumbled with the buttons on her ruffled shirt. Ricky wasn't wearing a bra, and they both made a low moaning sound the moment Alice touched her.

Zippers cooperated, and Alice's dress easily slipped to the floor beside white tuxedo pants and bikini underwear. There was a glimpse of longing in Ricky's eyes as Alice pushed the shirt off her shoulders and let it fall to the floor. Alice filled her hands with that marvelous blonde hair again, kissing her with such passion that Alice wasn't sure she would ever be able to stop. At that moment she wanted to hear Ricky's voice once more, that thrilling, tantalizing voice.

"You have no idea how much I want you," Ricky whispered. The huskiness made Alice tremble and caused that wonderful fluttering to start all over again. Their naked bodies were flushed and warm as Alice pulled her down on the bed and let herself be carried away in the magic of it all.

Ricky seemed to be everywhere, touching Alice where she needed to be touched and kissing her where she wanted to be kissed. There was never a question of who was in control once things got started. Alice was more than willing to let herself be ravished.

Ricky moved on top of her and took one of Alice's nipples into her mouth. Alice was already on the edge of orgasm when Ricky began moving slowly, deliberately down the length of her body, licking and sucking everywhere along the way. Alice loved the anticipation of it almost as much as the act itself. She had never let go so completely before, but she wanted this. She wanted everything this woman was willing to give her.

Alice's hands were in Ricky's hair again, and she opened her legs to Ricky's aggressive mouth kissing the inside of her thighs. Ricky wasted no time tasting and exploring the very core of her, and Alice spread her legs more and raised her hips to meet that insistent, probing tongue.

"Oh, yes . . ." Alice heard herself saying over and over in a voice she didn't recognize. Ricky pulled her closer with hands under hips, her tongue penetrating and subtle, her lips sucking, savoring hot pulsing flesh. Alice grabbed Ricky's head as a throbbing surge of heat began coursing through her body. Again Ricky's hands were everywhere, touching, pleasing, bringing Alice to the brink of rapturous delight. Alice came hard and threw her head back, her whole body shaking with sensation.

Finally Alice lay still, the only sound in the room coming from her labored breathing. Ricky slowly kissed her way back up Alice's trembling body and lingered over her breasts, nuzzling them with damp cheeks and teasing Alice's hard nipples before taking them in her mouth again one at a time.

"They're nice," she said as she touched Alice's

firm nipples with the tip of her tongue. "Very nice." She brushed her cheek against them and kissed Alice fully on the mouth. "God, you're nice everywhere." She gently nudged Alice with her chin. "Turn over. I need to feel all of you."

Alice obeyed and immediately began to purr as Ricky's warm, soft body covered hers and that mouth began making a path along the back of her neck. Alice could feel Ricky's hard nipples pressing against her and heard herself moan with pleasure the moment Ricky reached around to touch her breasts. Those hands seemed to be everywhere, and before Alice knew what was happening, fingers were slipping inside of her, taking her once more over the edge.

"You feel so good," Ricky whispered. "I wanted you the first night I saw you."

Those fingers worked more magic, and it wasn't long before Alice came again, thrashing around and moaning wildly. She finally stopped moving, but was grateful that the fingers stayed in place. She lay in a weak, sweaty heap, trying to get her breathing back to normal. The next thing she knew, Ricky was beside her brushing Alice's hair away from her face.

"You're beautiful," Ricky said. "Can I hold you?"

Alice managed to find enough strength to turn over. *Yes*, she thought. *Hold me. That's exactly what I want.* She sank into Ricky's arms and tried to laugh. "Give me a minute," she said shakily. "I feel as if I've been hit by a train."

Ricky moved another lock of hair away from Alice's eyes. "We'll pretend that's a compliment."

She nuzzled Alice's neck and nibbled at her

earlobe. As Alice regained her composure, she rolled Ricky on her back and kissed her. "I've thought about nothing but you for weeks now."

Ricky tilted her head back to encourage more of Alice's mouth on her throat. Alice kissed her everywhere she could touch . . . the soft hollow of her shoulder and the side of Ricky's firm, ample breast. "After lunch that day," Alice said, "I didn't want you to leave." She began moving against her in a slow grinding motion and then maneuvered a leg in between Ricky's legs where a welcome dampness awaited her.

Ricky searched Alice's face with serious blue eyes and kissed her chin and the corner of her mouth. "It usually takes me forever to come," she said in her low raspy voice.

"I'm in no hurry," Alice whispered, and then covered Ricky's mouth with her own. *I'm in no hurry.*

Alice woke up to the hint of morning seeping through the drapes and Ricky's hand possessively resting on her thigh. She squinted in the direction of the digital clock beside the bed and stretched lazily against the warm, sleeping body next to her.

Alice was certain that they couldn't have been asleep more than a few hours, although she didn't know what time it had been when they finally collapsed from exhaustion. With the memory of their lovemaking still fresh in her mind, Alice traced the back of her hand along the soft dimpled cheek and reached over and moved thick, shaggy hair away from Ricky's face.

"Good morning," Ricky croaked and snuggled up next to her.

Alice smiled at the early-morning sound of Ricky's voice — like someone in the beginning stages of laryngitis.

Ricky propped herself up on an elbow and slowly moved her hand from Alice's thigh to the wetness between her legs. "You were full of surprises last night."

"So were you." Alice opened her legs further and reached for Ricky's breast. "We've been at it for hours already and I still want you." She trembled as Ricky's tongue ran along the edge of her ear; she felt a tingle race up and down her arms.

Ricky made love to her slowly, with her mouth, her hands, her eyes, and that fascinating voice that Alice could never hear often enough. Alice answered with a kiss before letting herself be carried away in yet another flood of passion. *Who am I kidding? This is more than lust, idiot. I'm in love with her already.*

Ricky put her white ruffled shirt back on but didn't bother to button it, while Alice tugged on a terry cloth robe. Grumbling stomachs made food a priority.

"Was he mad?" Alice asked. She'd caught only one end of Ricky and Joe's earlier telephone conversation, and *mad* didn't begin to describe what she'd heard.

"He'll get over it," Ricky said. "Canceling a rehearsal is a big deal, but then so is this." She came up behind Alice, who was holding the refrigerator door open. Ricky kissed the back of her neck and put her arms around her. "It was the part about canceling *Sunday's* rehearsal too that really pissed him off." She chuckled and gave Alice a firm hug.

"So you can stay the whole weekend?" Alice asked. She couldn't have cared less how pissed off Joe Langley was. *I've got her for the whole weekend!*

"Is there anything to eat?" Ricky asked. They both peered into the virtually empty refrigerator. "We skipped dinner last night."

"Looks pretty bleak in here," Alice said, a bit embarrassed. "I don't cook much."

"Eggs and stale bread." Ricky started pulling things out and piling them on the counter. "And we can whittle the green stuff off this hunk of cheese." She kissed Alice on the cheek. "The emergency's over. An omelet's about to be born."

Alice propped her head up in her hand and watched Ricky finish her last bite of toast. They had returned to bed with their plates and devoured breakfast with little effort. Alice took their dishes and set them on the nightstand beside her. Ricky looked adorable in her ruffled shirt and a scrambled sheet tucked around her. She tossed a stray lock of hair away from her eyes and leaned back against a stack of pillows.

"So," Ricky said. "Would I be here now if I hadn't worn a tuxedo last night?"

"Oh, definitely," Alice said. "I should've insisted on this weeks ago, actually. The first time it occurred to me."

"Weeks ago?"

Alice reached over and touched the side of Ricky's face with the back of her hand. "Weeks ago," she whispered.

Ricky trembled and closed her eyes. Alice remembered a similar reaction last night the first time she had touched her.

"Let me make love to you again," Alice said quietly. Something was telling her to approach Ricky this way. *Go slow*, Alice thought. *For some reason she needs to know this is my idea.*

Their lovemaking the night before and earlier that morning had been almost totally one-sided. Ricky was an excellent lover, enthusiastic and passionate, but whenever Alice attempted to take control of the situation, she found herself in a new position and at the mercy of those incredible hands and that exquisite mouth. Only once had she been allowed to reciprocate.

Ricky leaned over and pulled the sash on Alice's robe. Her smile was enticing and playful as she slid down in the bed and opened Alice's robe farther. She reached over and took one of Alice's breasts in her hand, teasing the nipple with her thumb. But Alice sat up and slowly pulled the sheet away from Ricky's partially nude body.

"You first this time," she said, and with a hand behind Ricky's head, Alice brought her mouth down and kissed her hard. She was instantly rewarded with that little noise she loved to hear, the noise only a woman can make — that slight intake of breath that's not quite a sob but more than a sigh. Alice heard it and deepened the kiss by gripping a handful of Ricky's hair and pulling her closer.

The kiss turned wild for a moment, and Alice heard that sound again when her tongue touched Ricky's. The hint of uncertainty and mere trace of resistance that had been there earlier was suddenly gone as Ricky melted into her arms. They kissed for a long time and then Alice rolled on top of her and straddled her body. She got her robe off and opened Ricky's already unbuttoned shirt the rest of the way. Their eyes met, and Alice leaned over to kiss her again before moving slowly down Ricky's body with only one thing in mind. *You first this time.*

"When can I see you again?" Alice asked late Sunday night. They were by Alice's door and still inside the apartment. Alice's robe hung loose over her naked body as she draped the white coat around Ricky's shoulders and kissed her. "Are you off any this week?"

"No," Ricky said. "Our weekend gig was closed for maintenance. That's the only reason I didn't have to work last night." She slipped her hands inside Alice's robe. "And we're recording every day this week. Joe's got the studio booked. I can't get out of it."

"Are you working this weekend too?" Alice asked.

She could hear an edge of panic in her voice. Five days before seeing her again. This would never do.

"At Sugar Daddy's Friday and Saturday night," Ricky said. She sounded as disappointed as Alice felt.

"I don't know if I can wait that long," Alice said.

Ricky kissed her on the lips. "When we're recording, things can go on until really late sometimes, so during the week's impossible for me. As long as my voice holds up and we're all still awake, we keep working when we've got the studio."

"Then I'll be in Austin Friday night," Alice said. She ran her fingers through the front of Ricky's hair. "Five days is forever. I miss you already."

Ricky called her every night after she got in from the studio. She always sounded tired and apologized for the lateness of the hour.

"How'd it go?" Alice asked. It was Tuesday night and she was working late also. Alice's dining room table was full of paperwork relating to damage estimates from the storm in Harlingen. She had a meeting in Dallas at ten in the morning. She glanced at her watch and noted that it was already after eleven.

"It went so well they're all sort of edgy right now," Ricky said. Her voice sounded rough and raw, as though it might hurt for her to talk. "Joe says you can't mix women and music. Real relationships are too distracting. You can have one or the other, but you can't have both. So I'm working really hard to disprove his theory."

"He actually *told* you that?"

Ricky laughed. "He actually *believes* that."

"Then I'm probably not very popular with the band right now."

"They'll get over it."

On Wednesday afternoon Dora Martinez called Alice at the office. Alice had meant to get in touch with her earlier and apologize for leaving her and Marge stranded with Lola at the HRCF dinner.

"So what happened on Friday night? And why is your phone always busy?" Dora asked, getting right to the point.

Alice slowly swiveled around in her chair behind her desk, twisting the telephone cord with one hand. "The white tuxedo. I think I'm in love."

"Oh shit. Really?"

"Really." '

"That's great!"

Alice could hear her smacking her gum.

"Who is she?" Dora bellowed. "None of us had ever seen her before. And believe me, if we'd ever seen her before we wouldn't forget it."

"Her name's Ricky Conrad," Alice said. "Check with your kids. They've probably heard of her."

"I'll do that. Is everything else okay?"

"Everything's fine. Wonderful in fact."

"Right. Good. Then we'll chat more later."

Late Thursday morning Dora called her again. "Your Ricky Conrad," she said. "I couldn't find any dirt on her."

Alice was caught by surprise. "You checked her out?"

"Of course I checked her out. Your friends are worried about you."

"My friends need to mind their own business!"

"Come on, Alice. You know —"

"Who put you up to this?" Alice snapped. "Christine? Lola?"

"Your friends are worried about you," Dora said again. "I've gotta go. We'll chat more later."

Alice hung up, fuming, and had a good idea who was responsible. She called Christine Marlow for lunch and met her at an overpriced and understaffed bar and grill on the Saint Mary's Strip.

"What's the occasion?" Christine asked as they scanned their menus. "You're usually too busy for lunch."

"Dora called," Alice said, still angry at having her privacy invaded. "Was it your idea to have Ricky checked out?"

"Ricky? You mean the little blonde number you picked up the other night?"

Alice set her menu down. *What the hell's going on here?*

"There was reason for concern," Christine said. "You've been buried under your work ever since I've known you, Alice. We were interested in knowing what kind of woman had finally gotten your attention."

The waitress took their orders and swept their menus away.

"How old is she?" Christine asked. "She looks like jailbait from what I remember. And the pictures are —"

"Where did you get *pictures*?" Alice roared.

"One of those rocker magazines. *Spin, Slime,*

something like that. Dora showed us an article on her."

"Us? Who the hell is *us*?"

"Dora, Marge, and Lola. We're all worried about you."

Alice was too angry to eat or say much of anything else. She caught a glimpse of a white jacket draped over an arm and looked up quickly. A vivid memory of Ricky in a ruffled white shirt and nothing else made her stop and take a deep breath. Somewhere in the distance Alice could vaguely hear Christine talking.

Chapter Five

Friday evening Alice bought a Hot Check CD at the mall, hurried home to change clothes, and packed a bag for the weekend. She played the CD twice on the way to Austin. Hearing Ricky's voice was a rush, but it was nothing compared to the thought of seeing her again.

Having spent the last three years on nothing but making a success of the Restaurant Division of Collins Enterprises, Alice's work had become her passion. There hadn't been time for anything else, and her father expected that type of commitment from her. Until now Alice hadn't realized how much she had missed having a real life, but Ricky had changed all that in less than a week.

Once Alice arrived at Sugar Daddy's, Ricky spotted her and motioned toward a clean, empty table near the stage. The music was deafening, but Alice could see everything that was going on and had the best seat in the house.

Ricky was behind the keyboard, just a few feet from where Alice was sitting. She wore faded jeans torn at the knee, white sneakers, and a blue denim shirt with the top three buttons undone. Her voice was powerful, and the music fast and pulsating. The dance floor was filled with young, sweaty bodies as the Friday night crowd kept flowing into the club. Ricky changed instruments when that particular song was over and played guitar for the second half of a set. The band finally took a break about thirty minutes later.

Ricky jumped down from the stage and slipped into the leather jacket Stan gave to her. She leaned over and whispered in Alice's ear, "Come with me while I change clothes."

Alice gave her the small suitcase sitting in a chair and followed her down a hallway to an office in the back. Ricky found the light switch, locked the door behind them, and put her arms around Alice. Their first kiss in five days was a slow, deep exchange of tongues.

"It's better than I remembered," Ricky whispered. "How's that possible?" Kisses moved down Alice's throat to the top of her breasts and renewed the fluttering in Alice's stomach. Alice wanted to feel more of her and searched for Ricky's mouth again as she pulled her closer.

"My clothes are all wet," Ricky said.

Alice chuckled and kissed her on the forehead. "Mine are wet in a few places too. As a matter of fact, I don't think I've had dry underwear since I met you."

Ricky stripped and tugged on black leather pants and a white shirt. She stuffed her wet clothes in the suitcase and ran a towel through her damp hair. "I'll give you a key to my apartment and draw a map for you," Ricky said. "It's easy to find from here."

Alice leaned against the door and watched her get dressed, remembering how that body had felt on top of her last weekend. "I'd rather stay here at the club with you," Alice said.

Ricky looked over at her as she buttoned up her shirt. "It's so loud and smoky. Besides, you worked all day. Aren't you tired?" She smiled and tucked her shirttail in. "Trust me. You'll need your rest for later."

Alice liked the sound of that. "I've been resting for five long days." She was a lot of things at the moment — excited, thrilled, horny — but tired wasn't one of them.

Ricky stopped running the towel through her hair and draped it around her neck. Their eyes met and Alice whispered, "Come here."

Ricky was in her arms again, kissing her throat and giving Alice just a mere sample of how good it would be when they finally got out of there later.

They didn't break away from each other until Joe pounded on the door.

After Hot Check finished their last song for the night, the house lights came up and Ricky jumped down from the stage with her leather jacket already halfway on. "I need to change clothes again before we go."

"I'd better wait for you here," Alice said. She handed over the small suitcase and lowered her voice. "The next time I touch you I won't be able to stop."

Alice and the three other band members watched Ricky gracefully weave her way around tables, chairs, and straggling customers. Alice heard the snap of a guitar case closing before Joe came over to the table.

"Are you sure you know what you're doing?" he grumbled.

"Positive," Alice said.

"She plays for keeps. Just don't fuck her up."

He's worried about her, Alice thought as they continued glaring at one another.

"I helped put her back together once," he said. "I'm sure I can do it again if I have to." He picked up his guitar and walked out the door.

Stan came over to the table, winding up the cord to his bass. His beard was full and had a reddish tint to it. He looked down at Alice and chuckled. "Joey there don't like you much."

Alice briefly inspected her watery drink and drained it. "Really?"

He pulled out a chair and sat down. "Yeah, really. He hates it when he can't get Ricky's full attention. He likes her mind stayin' on her work." He laughed and checked the contents of two beer bottles on the table. "But he'll come around once he sees you're serious." He glanced over at her and scratched his beard. "You *are* serious, aren't you?"

Alice decided that his approach was a little smoother than Joe's, but Stan was out to accomplish the same thing. These two guys were like a pair of big brothers checking out a new suitor. In its own archaic way, it was almost sweet.

Ricky was already on her way back, having changed into black corduroy pants, a gray Hot Check T-shirt, and her black leather jacket. Alice was amazed at how good she could look in something so simple.

"Where's Joe?" Ricky asked.

"Outside pouting." Stan looked up at her and grinned. "Let me guess. No rehearsal tomorrow."

"Right. We worked hard all week. We deserve it." To Alice she said, "You ready?" Ricky threw Kyle, the drummer, a kiss and then reached over and tugged on Stan's beard. "I'll be here at seven forty-five tomorrow night. Try to have him in a better mood please."

Stan shrugged. "Maybe we can get him laid."

Alice followed Ricky to her apartment, which was indeed not far from Sugar Daddy's. The first thing she noticed when they arrived was a pleasant vanilla scent in the living room. At a glance Alice saw new black and white furniture, all tastefully futuristic. The apartment was big and neat, and Alice immediately felt comfortable there.

She slid her palms over the front of that soft leather jacket while Ricky kissed her throat and neck, leaving Alice almost too weak to stand on her own. She touched Alice's ear with the tip of her tongue before taking it into her warm, wet mouth. Alice's back was pressed against the door, and Ricky's hand had worked its way under her shirt to rub her breasts.

They helped each other out of their clothes. Ricky's jacket tumbled to the floor, and Alice pulled the T-shirt over her head. They quickly became a naked tangle of arms and legs on the carpet by the door.

"I need to touch you," Ricky whispered huskily. Her hand started at Alice's knee and slowly moved up her thigh. Ricky slipped two fingers inside her and teased Alice's nipples with a shake of her hair.

Deep feverish kisses resumed as Alice unconsciously raised her hips to meet the stroking. Ricky's tongue was in Alice's mouth matching the movements of her fingers, and she kissed Alice's neck and the side of her face moments before urging, whispering the words, "Help me make it good for you."

Alice could hear moaning and finally recognized it as her own. The kiss turned desperate as she sucked on Ricky's tongue and thrashed around, her body demanding more as the inevitable drew closer. She finally squeezed her legs together, trapping Ricky's fingers inside, wrenching the last ounce of pleasure from her hand. Alice pulled her mouth away and rubbed her cheek against the side of Ricky's face.

After a moment, Ricky leaned over and propped herself up on an elbow. "You sound so good when you come."

Alice pushed her gently to the carpet and rolled on top of her, her body settling easily on Ricky's body. Their mutual longing and desire was evident as Alice moved against Ricky. They'd both waited all week for this.

The next morning the telephone woke them. Ricky reached for it on the nightstand and mumbled something into the receiver. Alice pulled at the blanket to cover Ricky better and kissed her cheek before heading for the bathroom. Just as she got back, Ricky set the phone down.

"That was Joe checking to see if you were still here," she said. Her early-morning voice was hoarse and huskier than usual. Hearing it made Alice smile.

She spruced up the bed while Ricky was in the bathroom. *If these sheets could talk*, Alice thought as she smoothed the blanket and fluffed the pillows. Glancing around, she noticed a picture of the band near the telephone and picked it up. Ricky was standing between Kyle and Stan, with Joe behind them. Ricky looked the same, but the other three band members were much younger. Stan didn't have a beard in the picture, and Kyle and Joe were thinner with much longer hair.

Ricky came out of the bathroom and crawled back into bed, pulling Alice in beside her. "Munich five years ago," she said. "Our first world tour when we opened for Cosmic Blue. A nice little German man took it for us."

"Cosmic Blue," Alice said. She couldn't say for sure what songs Cosmic Blue sang, but she'd certainly heard of them. She reached over to put back the picture and smiled as Ricky moved into her arms.

"Did he really call to see if I was still here?" Alice asked, giving her a hug and kissing the top of her head.

"Ignore him," Ricky said. "He's just being an asshole." She tucked the blanket in around them. "Can I ask you something?" Her hand moved slowly back and forth across Alice's bare stomach, just below her breasts. "You don't have to answer since it's really none of my business."

"Ask away."

Ricky chuckled and cleared her throat. "Are you seeing anyone else right now?"

Alice shook her head. "No. What about you?"

"I'm so available it's almost embarrassing," she whispered. "I couldn't help but notice the women you were with the other night."

"They're just friends."

Ricky raised up a little and pushed her pillow under her head. "I'm glad to hear that. Can I ask you something else?" Not bothering to wait for a reply, she quietly asked, "You know that little thing you do on the edge of the bed sometimes? Who taught you how to do that?"

Alice turned on her side and propped her head up with her own pillow. "I dated a jock in college for a while. She taught me a lot of things."

"Thank her for me if you ever see her again."

Alice smiled. "I'll be sure and add a note in her Christmas card this year."

"Come here and let me hold you," Ricky said.

They rearranged the pillows and the blanket and got comfortable again.

"I have a bazillion questions to ask you," Ricky said as she slowly ran a finger along Alice's arm. "I'd like to know everything about you. I can already picture you as a kid. You probably had this little briefcase that you carried to day care."

Alice raised an eyebrow. "Putting my crayons in a backpack seemed tacky even then."

She answered each of Ricky's questions thoughtfully and found herself talking about an array of things, including her parents, Collins Enterprises, and restaurant management. An hour later over orange juice, coffee, and Pop-Tarts, they were still talking in the middle of the bed when the phone rang again.

"That's probably Stan," Ricky said. She handed Alice her empty glass and reached over to answer it. "Yes, she's still here," Ricky said without any further telephone etiquette. "We're having breakfast, and whatever it is you have to say right now can wait until I see you later." She hung up and squeezed Alice's hand. She held it and lightly traced a line on Alice's palm with a fingertip. "So tell me, Ms. Collins," Ricky whispered. "How old were you the first time you really carried a briefcase?"

Alice soon lived for weekends, and driving to and from Austin at all hours was certainly worth the inconvenience. Ricky had quickly become the center of Alice's entire life, and arranging time to be with her was a number one priority.

In addition to all the traveling Alice was doing, Ricky had the band's schedule adjusted so they'd be in San Antonio several times a month. Alice, in turn, juggled her own schedule to ensure that she could be in town on those days.

One Wednesday night at Muldoon's a few weeks later, Joe came over to Alice's table while Ricky was off changing clothes. Hot Check had just finished their first set.

"You're back," he said, and sat down next to her. "Why am I still surprised?"

Alice smiled at him innocently and said, "Because you're a jerk?"

Shock registered on his thin, handsome face before he laughed. "That's a Ricky Conrad word. What's she been saying about me?"

"That I should give you a little time to get used to this."

He leaned back in his chair. "Since it doesn't look like you're going away, I don't have much of a choice, do I?"

Stan came over with a round of drinks, gave Joe a beer, and set a gin and tonic down in front of Alice. With a slight grin he mumbled, "Ricky says we gotta be nice to you." He took a swig of his beer and then looked over several heads in the direction that Ricky should be coming from at any minute. "There're some guys waitin' for her by the dressing room," he said. "Kyle might need some help with 'em."

Alice and Joe watched him leave, and for the first

time she realized that the band's breaks had a definite routine. Part of that routine included watching out for Ricky.

"Is she having trouble with fans?" Alice asked.

"A few months ago she was practically mobbed at a club in Houston," he said.

"Mobbed? What happened?"

"Five or six guys with too much to drink caught her outside the dressing room. One of them wanted to dance with her and the others just wanted to talk, but they were very persistent. By the time Kyle got there, Ricky was surrounded by a snuff-toting gaggle of testosterone." Joe smiled. "Her words, not mine." He shrugged. "Ricky didn't give it much thought, but it really shook up the rest of us."

Alice scanned the crowd and zeroed in on the direction Stan had gone. The club and its patrons didn't seem quite so friendly any longer.

"We need to make sure she's careful," Alice said. "I'll talk to her about it."

Joe perked up a bit. "Thanks. Maybe she'll listen to you." He had a little smirk on his face as he took another sip of his beer. "I've been giving her a hard time about skipping rehearsals on weekends. I reminded her that she's never put a chick ahead of work before."

Alice bristled at the work *chick*. She hadn't heard the term used that way since junior high. *Christ, do guys still talk like that?*

"And what did Ricky say?" Alice asked.

Joe turned in his chair and propped his arm up on the back of it. "She told me never to call you a chick again." He chuckled and picked up his beer. "We can either use your name or refer to you as her *lover*. Not her friend and not her girlfriend. Her lover." He took another slow drink and said, "Not only do we have to watch out for the usual PC bullshit she insists on, but now we've gotta stay on top of these gay terms too."

Alice managed a smirk of her own. "She referred to me as her lover?" Just saying the word excited her.

"Yeah," he said seriously. "So far you're in a league all your own with that one. She's a babe in the woods when it comes to stuff like this, Alice. She might look like experience is her middle name, but that's not the case. Just don't screw her up. That's all I'm asking."

It was a simple request, and Alice could see that it was made by someone who truly cared about Ricky.

"Here she comes," he said. "As long as Ricky likes you, that's good enough for us. Believe me. When *she*'s not happy, nobody's happy."

Chapter Six

A week later early Saturday morning it was two-fifteen before Alice and Ricky left Sugar Daddy's. They'd been seeing each other for almost two months, and Alice was just as ready for her now as she'd been their first night together.

Ricky unlocked her apartment door and set her guitar down in the corner. She switched on a light that uncovered the chaos of the room; boxes were stacked everywhere, and the entertainment set that had been filled with stereo equipment and books the weekend before was gone.

"What's all this?" Alice asked in surprise. She glanced around more carefully, noticing the bare wall where the huge Joan Jett picture had previously hung. Ricky took her by the hand and led her to the bedroom. More boxes were stacked in a corner, and what little furniture was usually in the room was now moved against the wall.

Ricky kissed her on the neck and nibbled at her ear, but Alice was distracted by all the confusion.

"Why the boxes? Are you painting the apartment?"

"No," Ricky whispered as her mouth worked its way down Alice's throat. "I'm moving the band to San Antonio next week."

Alice's eyes flew open. "You're what?"

Ricky began unbuttoning Alice's shirt. "I'm moving."

Alice took Ricky's face in her hands and brushed thick hair away from her eyes. "Why didn't you tell me?"

Ricky avoided looking at her and shrugged. "I didn't know how you'd feel about it. And nothing could happen anyway until Joe found us a permanent gig there."

"Has he done that?" They'd stopped undressing each other. Alice took Ricky by the hand and led her to the edge of the bed.

"Friday and Saturday nights at a club called Sneakers," Ricky said. "We start in two weeks. He's working on a few other things too."

We'll finally be together! She wanted to grab her and hug her, but Ricky's lack of enthusiasm held her back.

"When can you move?" Alice asked.

"This week." Ricky pulled off a brown suede boot and dropped it on the floor. "I've called on a few apartments already, but the boys are looking for a house somewhere outside of town. We need a place to rehearse."

She wants her own apartment, Alice thought, her heart sinking. The other boot hit the floor, and Ricky gently pushed Alice back on the bed.

"You're getting your own apartment?" Alice said. She was hurt and didn't care whether or not Ricky heard it in her voice.

"Yes. My own apartment. I certainly can't live with the boys. They're pigs." She leaned over Alice and began unbuttoning the rest of her shirt. Their eyes met, and Alice detected a flicker of vulnerability, a moment of fear etched in her expression. "And I certainly can't live with you," Ricky said.

"Why not?" Alice whispered.

Ricky's hand stopped moving along Alice's warm, bare skin. "Because you've never asked me to," she said huskily. She moved on top of her, straddling Alice's body, causing that familiar roller coaster tumbling to start all over again in Alice's stomach.

Alice reached up and finished unbuttoning Ricky's shirt and slowly ran her palms over cool, soft flesh. She was afraid of sounding too needy or desperate, but the thought of having Ricky with her in San Antonio on a permanent basis was thrilling.

"My not asking you is only a technicality," Alice said.

Ricky's shirt came off and was tossed somewhere on the other side of the room. That shaggy hair fell to her bare shoulders, and those blue eyes settled on

Alice easily. She took Alice's hands and laced their fingers together.

"But a very important technicality," Ricky said. "You mean more to me than just a good fuck, so don't even dream of suggesting that we live together unless it's what you really want."

Alice took Ricky's firm nipples between her fingers and rubbed them slowly with her thumbs. "Oh, I want it all right. I'm in love with you. I thought you knew that."

"Oh, Jesus," Ricky said, her smile radiant. "I'm in love with you too. How did that happen?" She leaned over and kissed her, and then nuzzled Alice's neck playfully.

Alice pulled her closer and whispered, "Am I really a good fuck?"

Ricky's low chuckle certainly made her want to be.

Alice's place wasn't big enough for two, so she found them a huge condo on the north side of town and helped coordinate Ricky's part of the move first.

"I haven't had a vacation in five years," Ricky said as she began unpacking boxes. The band had a week off before their new gig started. Alice helped her get things settled before her own part of the move began. It was exciting as well as exhausting, but they both seemed determined to get some sort of order back into their lives.

"When do I get to see where the boys live?" Alice asked one Saturday morning in early November.

They'd just finished taking a shower together and briefly discussed whether or not to go out for breakfast. "Don't you have a rehearsal later?"

"At eleven," Ricky said. Her voice was little more than a croak. Alice liked the way it sounded when she first woke up.

They pulled on huge Hot Check T-shirts and padded to the kitchen to see if there was anything to eat.

"Looks like we're having French toast and sausage if we stay home," Ricky said. "Oh, and there's some leftover fettuccine alfredo from the other night."

"Sounds great," Alice said. "Let's fix it all." She'd already decided against breakfast out. "I'll get the coffee going. There's orange juice in the freezer."

Fifteen minutes later breakfast was ready; the fettuccine tasted better than it had the first time around.

"Can I go with you today?" Alice asked. "I've never been to a rehearsal before."

"It's pretty boring," Ricky said. "We may be working on the same song all day."

"Is that a no? I promise to be quiet. You won't even know I'm there."

Ricky tilted her head and looked at her. "You really wanna go? Sometimes I yell a lot. It might not be pretty."

"Mmm. I like forceful women. You didn't answer my question. Can I go? Will the boys mind if I'm there?"

"No, they won't mind." Ricky picked up their breakfast dishes and took them to the kitchen. "Maybe you should take your car in case you change your mind once you're there."

Not only did Alice stay for the entire rehearsal, but she spent at least an hour talking to Stan and Kyle about the band's new gig at Sneakers and Ricky's two new songs they were working on. Alice could hear Joe's guitar in the other room and Ricky on keyboards going over a riff she wasn't happy with. Stan and Kyle were taking a break until they were needed again.

"She's been comin' up with some damn good stuff lately," Kyle said. It was the longest sentence Alice had ever heard him say. He pulled at the end of his bushy mustache and shook his head. "Some *damn* good stuff."

"We're two songs away from another album," Stan informed her. "She's crankin' it out faster than we can put it together."

"You mean her work has got better since she fell in love with me?" Alice asked innocently.

Kyle and Stan both cut their eyes over at her. Kyle threw his head back and laughed while Stan mumbled, "Yeah, somethin' like that."

A while later, the music in the living room stopped, and Joe came to the door and motioned for the other two. Alice followed Stan and Kyle into the other room and waved at Ricky, who was behind the keyboard. Stretching out on the couch where she'd been earlier in the day, Alice adjusted her position to give her the best view of Ricky.

"You're still here," Ricky said. Alice could tell by her smile that she was glad to see her.

"I've been hanging out with the band," Alice said.

"The really boring part's coming up," Ricky warned. "Let's take it from the top." She pointed to Kyle. "Come in with that boom-chucka beat again. I think it'll work in the beginning too. I liked it earlier."

As Alice listened to her and watched Ricky's hands move over the keyboard, she felt a familiar stirring between her legs. They'd made love that morning in the shower, but Alice wanted her again already, as though it had been weeks instead of hours since they'd been together. *Watching her play does this to me,* Alice realized for the first time. *My hormones start tap dancing the minute I see her touch the keyboard.*

This along with her sudden insight that listening to Ricky give the boys instructions had the same effect on her, was a revelation. Alice was even more aware of just how powerful Ricky's hold on her was. *She plays a note and I'm ready to drag her off to bed,* Alice thought. *She orders three guys around and I'm squirming on a stranger's sofa. What's the deal here?*

Alice quietly watched and listened as Ricky helped them shape the song into something that only she had been able to hear before. By three-thirty that afternoon, the rough edges were gone and a finished product was well on its way.

"Do we have lyrics yet?" Kyle asked. He twirled a drumstick through long, nimble fingers and flipped the switch on Joe's amplifier.

"Yeah," Ricky said. "We'll run through the whole thing tomorrow." She reached for Alice's hand and brought it to her lips for a kiss. "You either didn't get bored or you lost your car keys. Which is it?"

Alice pulled her key ring from her khaki shorts and held it up for inspection.

"It was kinda nice having you here today," Stan said to Alice. "Ricky didn't yell as much. Come back any time."

One Monday evening Alice came home to classical music on the stereo and a savory pot roast for dinner only minutes away from being ready. She found Ricky in the kitchen putting the finishing touches on two stuffed baked potatoes. The ends of her hair were still damp from her shower.

"It smells good in here," Alice said as she slipped her arms around her. The strawberry scent of Ricky's hair almost made her forget how hungry she was.

"Do we have plans for Thanksgiving?" Ricky asked after they sat down at the table. "It's this week, you know."

"I usually spend it with Dora and Marge. We're both invited this year."

"My father expects me to go to Austin," Ricky said, "but I'm not ready to deal with him yet. I was wondering if we could have something here. Just me, you, and the boys."

"The turkey and everything?" Alice asked. The hassle of a big dinner didn't appeal to her at all. "I guess we could have it catered. Or I can get my chef downtown to —"

Ricky's laughter caught her by surprise. "I'll do all the work," Ricky said. "It'll be fun. We'll go shopping for all the stuff tomorrow. How about it? Can we invite the boys over?" She scooped another helping of corn on her plate and waited patiently for

Alice's reply. "Or we can spend Thanksgiving with Dora and Marge. Either way's fine. It's your Thanksgiving too."

This is important to her, Alice thought. *And she's probably right — it might even be fun.*

"Just remember that I don't know anything about turkeys," Alice said. "Or cooking. If it doesn't come in a box, I can't even fake it."

Wednesday night before Thanksgiving Ricky had Alice and the boys there to help with the preliminaries. They chopped endless bowls of celery, onion, and bell pepper while Ricky baked pan after pan of cornbread. The chatter around the table easily kept Alice's attention. The band members liked bringing up embarrassing on-stage incidents, but Stan was the first to start with the road stories.

"Ricky's got these little rules when we're on the road," he said to Alice. "We've gotta stop for turtles in the highway and take turns getting them across to the other side."

"No matter what the traffic situation is," Joe said.

"And it never fails," Kyle added. "When it's my turn to tote them turtles, those little bastards end up pissing all over me."

"Turtle piss stinks, too," Joe confirmed. "It's all we can do to let him back in the van."

"And she's got this other rule," Stan said.

"I think Alice has heard enough by now," Ricky said. "And I can't believe we're sitting here talking about turtle piss."

As the night wore on, Alice's throat began to ache

from laughing so much. The band had a history together that they were willing to share with her, and Alice liked being a part of it. By midnight the chopping, baking, slicing, and dicing were all finished.

"Tomorrow morning starts the real work," Ricky said with her hands on her hips. She reached over and slapped Kyle on the back. "You guys done good. Be back here no later than eleven tomorrow. We're eating at noon."

Thursday night after two rounds of a turkey dinner, the boys were gone and the last dish was washed. Alice prepared a hot bubble bath for them and convinced Ricky to quit for the evening. Ricky had been up cooking since six that morning but still seemed to be holding up well.

"Football all day long," Ricky said as she slowly sank into the hot, foamy water. "Not just regular football, but *college* football. Double boring." She leaned her head back against the edge of the tub and closed her eyes. "This feels so good it's probably a sin."

Alice could feel Ricky's foot rubbing along her ribs. It was nice just being still for a change. Alice smiled to herself and didn't mind admitting that this was the best Thanksgiving she'd ever had. The boys weren't anything like what she'd expected.

"Kyle taught me a new card game," Alice said. "It's called Spit." Ricky's low, husky laughter made Alice smile. She jiggled her foot and splashed bubbles on Ricky's chin. "Don't get sleepy. I've got plans for you later."

They eventually got out of the tub and wrapped themselves in huge towels.

"How many relationships have you had?" Alice asked as she moved around behind her in the bedroom and kissed Ricky's bare shoulder.

"Three," Ricky said. "Actually, a big one in high school and two one-night stands on the road in Kansas a few summers ago. I don't get out much."

"Three? That's it?"

"You're disappointed."

"I'm surprised." She pulled Ricky's towel loose and let it fall to the floor. "Tell me about her. The one in high school."

"Emily was older than me," Ricky said. "An English teacher my sophomore year." She kissed Alice's throat and ran her hands over smooth, soft skin.

"Your first lover was a teacher?" Alice said. "Did she seduce you?"

"I was a willing participant. During the summer we'd spend all day together," Ricky said. "I'd leave her house at about five and go rehearse with the band for a few hours and then go home."

She ran a fingertip over one of Alice's hard nipples. Alice kissed her on the cheek and felt the heat beginning to smolder between her damp legs.

"One morning in August just before my senior year, Emily was packing when I got to her house," Ricky said. "She claimed to be going to California for a little vacation. Two months later there was a postcard in my mailbox saying she wouldn't be back. That was the last time I ever heard from her."

Alice brushed thick blonde hair away from Ricky's forehead. "That must've been rough," she said. Ricky

70

kissed her and then lowered her head to gently tug on Alice's nipple with her lips.

"You first tonight," Alice whispered before she got too caught up in the moment. Her tongue grazed Ricky's ear before she whispered, "Tell me what you want."

"I want you," Ricky said. "Open your legs for me."

Alice kissed her throat and then moved her mouth back up to Ricky's ear again. "You first this time. Please, baby. Tell me what you want. Talk to me." She took Ricky's full breast in her hands and could feel her trembling. "You like this?"

Ricky didn't say anything, but her slow, deep breathing gave her away.

"You do," Alice said. "I can hear it." She brushed her thumbs over hard nipples and kept her lips close to the edge of Ricky's mouth. "It doesn't take you forever to come any more, does it?"

Ricky chuckled and closed her eyes. "No. Not anymore."

Alice kissed her bare shoulder and neck again. "Tell me what you want, baby. Talk to me."

As their breathing became a bit more labored, Alice felt such a wonderful surge of arousal.

"Inside," Ricky whispered. "Go inside me."

Ricky was so wet that Alice thought she herself might come just from touching her. "Like this?" Alice said as her fingers slid in and out of her. She eased Ricky on the bed and slowly began to fuck her. "Like this?" Alice said again, knowing exactly what Ricky wanted.

Weeks ago Alice had discovered that Ricky was more sexually responsive when they talked while they made love. If Alice described an act just before doing it, the results were very rewarding.

"You like it this way, don't you?" Alice whispered. "You like it."

"Yes . . . yes."

Alice kissed her hard and Ricky opened her mouth for Alice's tongue. She came quickly and Ricky was like a limp rag afterward.

"Hold me," she said in a small, gravelly voice. "Hold me."

Alice kissed her on the cheek and still kept her fingers inside. Ricky nuzzled her neck as Alice's arms tightened around her.

"It was Emily, wasn't it?" Alice asked as she slipped her fingers out of her. "Emily's the one who mentioned how long it takes for you to come."

Ricky kissed the back of Alice's hand. "She stayed busy a lot. There were always papers to grade. You know. Teacher stuff."

"She would rather grade papers than make love to you?" Alice asked incredulously. She smoothed a lock of hair away from Ricky's eyes. "Was she out of her mind?"

Ricky turned on her side and propped her head up with her hand. "I was sixteen and eager to please. You're the first lover I ever had who wanted to make love to me. I feel like the luckiest damn person in the world right now." Ricky moved on top of her and Alice ran her hands up and down her back. "But I will admit," Ricky said, "that the first few times we were together in the beginning, whenever you'd start touching me, the thought would pop in my head — what if I can't come right away? What if it takes me a long time?" Ricky leaned over and kissed her. "Is it the kind of thing you apologize for? Do you warn someone you're about to sleep with that sometimes sex doesn't work for you?" She slipped her knee in between Alice's legs and slowly started moving against her.

"What about now?" Alice asked. "Do you still feel that way?"

"Things are a lot different now," Ricky said. "With the others I had sex; with you I have love. The difference is staggering."

Alice reached around and rubbed Ricky's sweaty back.

"And with you," Ricky whispered, "I seem to come quite often."

Chapter Seven

The week before Christmas Alice received an unexpected visit from Henry Conrad, Ricky's father. She had her secretary cancel an appointment so they'd have some time together. Gloria seemed to be checking him out when Alice met him outside her office. He was a young fifty, tall and fit, with light brown hair laced with gray and a very defined, handsome face. Ricky had his blue eyes, but other than that she didn't look anything like him.

"Please have a seat," Alice said graciously. She

motioned toward the chair in front of her desk. "May I get you something? We always have fresh coffee."

"No, thanks. I'm fine."

He was comfortable in his suit, as though he wore one often, and Alice could tell that he knew how good he looked. Ricky had indicated on several occasions that there was some tension between her and her father. Alice was aware that Ricky was still annoyed about his recently marrying a woman close to Ricky's age. Ricky's mother had only been dead a few years, and Ricky felt like it was much too soon for him to be trotting off with another woman.

"I understand from Joe that you and Ricky are living together," he said, coming right to the point.

"Yes. We're lovers," Alice replied, making a point of her own. "And I know for a fact that Ricky's told you all about that. You didn't hear it from Joe at all."

He met her steady gaze and then slowly looked away.

"She calls when she knows we won't be home," he said, "and she's never given me her telephone number or her new address. She can't possibly still be upset about Sharon and me getting married." He stopped abruptly and took a deep breath. "But that's not why I'm here. I'd like to invite you and Ricky to Austin for Christmas. The boys too, of course."

Alice didn't quite know what to say. She and Ricky had reservations at a resort in Vermont for the holidays. "I'll ask Ricky to call you," she said.

The look he gave her was intended to intimidate, but Alice wasn't impressed. When he saw that it wasn't working, he said, "You'll ask her to *call* me?"

"Better yet," Alice said, "let me see if I can get her on the phone for you now." She buzzed her secretary and had her put the call through. Their only chance to catch Ricky at rehearsal was if the band was taking a break, otherwise no one would be able to hear the phone ringing.

"How'd you find me?" Alice asked him.

"I've heard the commercial she did for you. It was easy from there." Henry shifted in the chair. "My daughter and I have had our differences over the years, but we've always been able to work them out." He spread his fingers and inspected his nails. "She's a classically trained pianist — a child prodigy who discovered rock 'n' roll at the age of ten. I wasn't happy with her choice of music, but we reached a compromise once I realized I couldn't change her mind. Then there's the Dentac Advertising Agency. They offered her an outrageous sum of money several years ago to join their staff. She said no, and we got over that one too. Her sexual orientation, her obsession with that teacher in high school, her —"

"You knew about the teacher?"

Henry's slight smile caught Alice's attention. He seemed very pleased with himself.

"As soon as I found out about the affair I suggested to Emily that she seek other employment before the school board put an end to her career. She left town the next day and Ricky adjusted."

Alice checked her anger and cleared her throat before testing her voice. "Did Ricky know you'd spoken to Emily?"

His eyes widened for a moment, and the smugness disappeared. "No. Of course not. She was sixteen. A minor. That woman was in a position of —"

"Yes, I know all that."

"You're not a parent," he said. "Ricky claims she's been a lesbian all her life, but at sixteen what can anyone know about their sexuality?"

"You didn't know about yours at sixteen?" Alice asked. She did notice, however, how easily he had said the word *lesbian*. She had to give him some credit for that. Alice could only imagine the conversations around the Conrad dinner table after Ricky came out to him years ago. *She's one up on me in that department.*

"Do you think it's fair the way she's treating my new wife?" he asked. "Sharon's very upset by all this. We were expecting the band home for Thanksgiving."

"I can't speak for Ricky on any of that," Alice said. "It's something the two of you will have to work out."

Alice's telephone buzzed, and Gloria let her know that Ricky was on the phone. Alice pushed a button, handed the receiver to him, then left him alone in her office.

Ricky declined her father's invitation for a Texas Christmas, and the holiday in Vermont helped recharge their batteries. Alice felt rested and ready for the new year. They were invited over to Dora and Marge's house for a New Year's Eve party, but Ricky had to work that night and would only be able to stay for an hour or so. By the time they got there, a roomful of lesbians were already well on their way to having a good time. Alice gave Ricky a small glass of orange juice and reached for her other hand.

77

"Where's your band playing tonight?" Dora asked over the noise of the crowd.

"Alamo Plaza," Ricky said.

Alice smiled at the expression on Dora's face. Alamo Plaza was *the* place to be on New Year's Eve. Tickets had been sold out for weeks already.

Lola and Christine came over with drinks in hand. They both gave Alice a hug.

"Christine's new squeeze is off flying the friendly skies," Lola said, "so she's a little grouchy right now." Lola gave Ricky a very thorough once-over, from the top of her shaggy blonde head to the toes of her brown suede boots.

"I thought for sure you'd be here in a tux," Lola cooed. "That's the only reason I came tonight."

"Sorry to disappoint you," Ricky said.

"Oh, honey," Lola sighed dramatically and began fanning herself with a plump hand. "That voice. Alice, darling, you'd better keep a close eye on this one."

Christine seemed to be severely annoyed about something, and Alice attributed her foul mood to having her new girlfriend out of town over the holidays. Christine finally crossed her arms over her chest and glared at both of them.

"Do you have a job?" she asked Ricky finally. "Do you work anywhere?"

"I need to be getting to work now, as a matter of fact," Ricky said. "I'm on in an hour."

"I mean at a real job," Christine said. "The power suit, morning traffic, a one-hour-lunch real job."

"She's an artist," Dora bellowed. "Artists don't wear power suits. What's the matter with you?

78

When's that girlfriend of yours coming back? You're more fun when she's in town."

"Oh, sit on it, Dora," Christine grumbled.

Ricky squeezed Alice's hand and leaned over to whisper that she needed to leave. Alice put her arms around her neck and kissed her.

"Don't forget," Alice said. "We've got a date when you get home later."

"I'm counting on it."

Alice was a wreck when she and Ricky went to Dallas a few weeks later to see Alice's parents. They flew out on a Wednesday afternoon to have dinner with them.

"Take it easy," Ricky said from her aisle seat. She gave Alice's hand a placating pat. "I promise not to embarrass you."

"I'm not worried about you." Alice ordered a gin and tonic to help settle her nerves. "I should've told them about me years ago. Why can't I do it? Who I sleep with should have nothing to do with them."

"You'll know when you're ready. Calm down. It's just dinner. We're not announcing our engagement or anything."

Alice lost what little courage she'd gained on the way up and introduced Ricky to her parents as a close friend, the writer and singer responsible for the commercial that was still making them barrels of money. Almost immediately Alice had envisioned her parents knowing every intimate detail of her personal life with no more than a glance at the two of them together. Alice unconsciously compensated for this by ignoring Ricky most of the evening. *I'm such a coward. This is the woman I love.* But no matter how reasonable she tried to be, Alice wasn't ready to come out to them yet. And she was grateful that Ricky didn't tease her about it. *This is nuts. What the hell are we doing here?*

The four of them had dinner at the country club, and early in the evening Alice realized that her father was positively enchanted with Ricky. He asked questions about her band and the videos she'd done. He told her how impressed he'd been with the jingle she'd written for them.

At that point Ricky casually mentioned that her band had been approached by another restaurant chain also wanting a jingle. The chain, however, just happened to be in direct competition with the restaurants owned by Collins Enterprises.

Alice was surprised by this and glanced at her father quickly as she set her fork down. To Ricky she said, "You won't do it, of course."

Ricky's eyes actually twinkled as she sliced a tomato chunk in her salad. "Why shouldn't I?" Her voice was soft and low, its huskiness so sensual when she spoke that way.

"Because I don't want you to," Alice said. It was only after her parents burst out laughing that Alice even attempted a smile. She saw absolutely nothing funny about any of it.

"Tell me, Alice," she heard her father saying. "What do you plan on doing about this? Ricky's apparently good enough to ruin us if she puts her mind to it."

"I'm not sure she's *that* good," Alice said. She could feel Ricky's eyes on her, and looked up in time to see her smile. Her mother wasn't saying much, but Alice could tell by the way she dabbed the napkin to her lips that things were going very well. *They like her,* Alice thought suddenly. She looked at both of her parents with surprise. *They like her a lot.*

After that particular visit, Alice's parents made it a point to always ask about Ricky whenever Alice called them or went up there for business. Coming out to them wasn't that far down the road, but Alice wasn't quite ready to get there yet. She wanted a few more profitable quarters on the books first.

Alice was home from the office early, but she still had some calls to make and a contract to look over. She could hear Ricky working in another room and noticed Joe's empty guitar case in the middle of the sofa. The music filtering through the door wasn't loud. Ricky usually worked on new material with only the bare necessities: a small keyboard, Stan and Joe on acoustic guitars, and occasionally Kyle smacking at bongos when he wasn't reading a magazine. As a piece progressed, more serious instruments were eventually incorporated and rehearsals moved to the boys' place on the outskirts of town.

Alice made her phone calls and jotted notes for her secretary. Ricky didn't have to work tonight and had hinted earlier that it would be nice if Alice could come home at a reasonable hour. Alice had to attend a board meeting in Dallas later in the week, and would be out of town for a few days. Her father was thinking about buying a department store chain in New Orleans and wanted her opinion on it.

The door to the music room opened and Joe came out carrying his guitar. "Your woman's a fuckin' genius," he said as he gently set his guitar in its case.

Alice put her pen down and propped her chin up on laced fingers. She watched him for a moment as the music continued from the other room.

"You hear that?" he said as he nodded toward the closed door. "She's working on something really hot, Alice." He tugged on the bill of his baseball cap and glanced at his watch. "I've gotta go. I'm late for an appointment." He left with his guitar, and Alice stayed where she was for a while listening to Ricky play. She thought twice about going in and curling up in the chair beside her. Watching Ricky work never failed to get her incredibly aroused.

Alice put the finished contract in her briefcase and quietly opened the door to Ricky's makeshift studio. The sound was full and mellow inside. Amplifiers and guitars of every shape and size lined three walls around the room. Cords and cables were neatly coiled and stacked in a corner. Ricky glanced over her shoulder and smiled as her hands continued moving across the keys.

"Hey," she said. "You're home early."

Alice came up behind her and draped her arms around Ricky's neck. "You promised to make it worth my while." She kissed her on top of the head and ran her hands down over the front of her shirt.

"We've got time for a bubble bath before dinner's ready."

"Mmm," Alice whispered as she nuzzled that sweet-smelling neck. "All of this and she cooks too."

PART TWO

Six Months Later

Chapter Eight

Alice and Ricky had an early dinner at one of the restaurants owned by Collins Enterprises and had plans to meet some friends later. The lighting at the restaurant was dim, the carpet plush. They enjoyed the best table available, with food cooked to perfection. Ricky signed a few autographs for customers; she was quickly becoming more than a local celebrity. Hot Check's music could be heard on all rock stations throughout the country, and Ricky was constantly being approached for interviews and fund-raisers. Their new album had two songs moving swiftly through the Top One Hundred.

"What are the boys doing on their night off?" Alice asked. After a half shake she stopped salting her baked potato, momentarily delighted by the sight of Ricky's tanned face and blue eyes in the candlelight. Ricky's hair had its usual semiorganized look about it. A look, however, that had been known to stop traffic on occasion.

"A baseball game somewhere, I think." Ricky focused her attention on her plate. "Are you sure this is a good idea? Some of your friends aren't that thrilled about us, you know."

"Don't be silly," Alice said. "Dora's one of your biggest fans."

Ricky laughed and nodded. "I'm not that worried about Dora. She doesn't seem to fit in with these women either. There's not a lot to be said for lowering your standards, Al, and that's what a few of them think you've done. I have nothing in common with these people. It's like comparing Streisand with Cindy Lauper. Or fondue with Cheez Whiz."

"I happen to love Cheez Whiz," Alice reminded her with a laugh.

After dinner they drove to Christine Marlow's house for a small party. "Come in. Come in," Christine said, giving Alice a hug. Her outfit consisted of beige pants with silver sparkling threads intricately woven into slightly puffed sleeves on the jacket. Christine's dangling earrings looked like small swaying chandeliers, and they matched a necklace that dipped into cleavage. "I see you brought the lounge singer."

Alice squeezed Ricky's hand as they followed Christine down the hallway.

"A lounge singer," Ricky grumbled. "See? She thinks you're keeping me, for crissake."

"Forget it for now, darling. I'll take care of her later." Alice smiled and hugged Dora. "How are you? I called you last week, but you were out of town. How are the kids?"

"They're fine," Dora said. She gave Ricky a hug too, and kept an arm around both of them. "How's the band? I hear you have a new album out."

They mingled and gossiped, with everyone sipping drinks. Lola Colby joined the three of them at the bar.

"Still no tux?" Lola asked as she handed Ricky an orange juice on the rocks.

"Alice only lets me wear it at home."

"She's a smart woman," Lola said. She propped herself up against the bar as close as she could get to Ricky. "Your voice is so . . . so . . . what's the word I'm looking for?"

"Sexy?" Alice offered.

"Yes! Sexy. That's it. Goodness, it's wonderful!"

Alice put her arm around Ricky's waist and ran her fingers through the front of her hair. "It is wonderful, isn't it?"

Dora was beside them, her martini-induced laughter bringing smiles to all. "Is that piano of yours tuned, Christine?" she yelled across the room.

"Of course it's tuned," Christine barked back. She couldn't have sounded more offended if someone had asked if her toilets flushed.

"Maybe Ricky'll play something for us," Dora said.

"A command performance! I've never heard her by herself."

Alice's hand moved down Ricky's back in a slow, lingering caress. She leaned closer and whispered, "Does my lounge singer feel like performing?" Their eyes met again and Ricky laughed.

"I'll play anything you'd like to hear."

Alice turned to the others, eyeing Christine in particular. "My little lounge singer can play anything you'd like to hear." Everyone followed them into another room through the French doors.

As Ricky played, the others stood around the piano drinking, singing, and giggling. The women made a game of trying to name songs Ricky didn't know, and it was a triumph when such a song was discovered. They had loosened up, taken off their shoes, and literally let their hair down. By one-thirty they were all tipsy and singing at the top of their lungs.

"It's late," Alice said a while later as she squinted at her watch. "I hope you can get us home."

"The wee hours of the morning are my specialty," Ricky said. "Stay right here while I get our things."

Alice and Dora huddled together against the piano and struggled to get their shoes on, but a commotion in the hallway got everyone's attention.

"She'll be tired of you in six months," Alice heard Christine say.

"That's what you told me six months ago," Ricky replied.

The others began filtering out into the hallway to see what was going on. They found Christine waving a finger in Ricky's face. "She can't possibly be in love with you," Christine said. She stumbled a little closer. "Six months. I'll give it another six months."

"You'll give what another six months?" Alice asked with a crinkled brow.

"It's not important," Ricky said. "You ready?" She put her arm around Alice and kissed the end of her nose. "You'll be asleep before we get out of the driveway. As the only sober person in the house," Ricky announced, "I think it's a good idea if I drive the rest of you home."

Alice rested her head on Ricky's shoulder. "She'll give what another six months?" she asked sleepily.

"Her new hair color," Ricky whispered. "Now come on. Lean against me and let's go."

And with that, Alice got an outrageous case of the giggles and couldn't even pull herself together long enough to tell Christine good-bye. Ricky helped Alice and Dora out the door first and put them safely in the car before returning for Marge and Lola. Alice was still giggling when Ricky finally got them home.

Monday morning Gloria made reservations for Alice at her restaurant on the Riverwalk. Alice arrived early for lunch, taking time to go through the kitchen and chat with employees. The manager seemed relaxed and undisturbed by her presence, which Alice found refreshing.

Christine was on time and dressed in dark blue slacks, a light blue silk blouse, and a matching jacket. "We haven't done this in a while," Christine said. "It's nice to see you in the daylight. What's the occasion?"

Alice folded her hands on the table. "I've been wanting to talk to you about Ricky."

Christine gave her a long, interested look, her eyes drifting to the top of Alice's fawn-colored blouse. "Trouble in paradise?"

The waiter brought their drinks and took their orders for lunch. Alice squeezed the lime into her iced tea and stirred vigorously. "You and I are friends, Christine," she started, "and I'd like for us to stay that way, but if you ever talk to Ricky the way you did the other night, I'll never speak to you again." She noticed a definite droop at the corner of Christine's mouth.

Christine set her glass down and stared at Alice in total disbelief. "Aren't you overreacting a little?"

"I don't think so," Alice said. "What has Ricky ever done to you? What the hell's your problem?"

"I couldn't even begin to explain." Christine picked up her glass and then nervously patted her already perfect hair. "She's not right for you, Alice. Everyone but you can see it."

"Who do you think you are?"

"I can't believe you," Christine roared. "She's making a *fool* out of you! She travels with three *men*. Three long-haired, doped-up *men*. How can you live with someone like that?"

It seemed strange hearing Joe, Stan and Kyle referred to as men. They were the boys. *She's talking about the boys!*

"You know absolutely nothing about her," Alice said, trying to keep her voice calm. "You're judging her by what her band looks like, and you know nothing about them either. You treat her like a gigolo, when she makes more money than *you* do! I don't understand any of this. I've never known you to be so relentless."

Christine's jaw was set, acknowledging a rage that Alice had only seen a few times. "It's no secret that I'm in love with you, Alice," she said through clenched teeth. "Seeing you with that blonde piece of fluff is almost more than I can bear."

"Oh, puleeze," Alice said. "You've never been in love a day in your life!"

"Ask anyone who knows me!" Christine spoke with such self-assurance that Alice had to look away from her. "I remember the first day I saw you. It was the most marvelous day of my life. I've wanted you for years, and you chose her over me. How can you expect me to be civil under these circumstances?"

Alice was mortified. She felt confused. Insensitive. *We're friends, for crissake,* she reminded herself. *We've been friends for years!*

"She's not right for you," Christine continued. "You're from different worlds."

Their food arrived, but neither acknowledged its existence. Alice was speechless. *How in the hell did I get myself into this one?* She pushed her plate away. "I really don't know what to say. I'm not even sure I believe you."

"What do I have to gain by lying to you? I know you've never been attracted to me. I've sensed your resistance from the beginning."

Alice forced herself to look at Christine, trying to get some sort of perspective on what their friendship had actually been all these years.

"I didn't mean to spring this on you," Christine said. "It just seemed important that you understand my position. Even under different circumstances I don't think Ricky and I could've become friends. The only thing we have in common is you."

Alice ran a fingertip through the sweat on her glass.

"Just remember what I've told you," Christine said. "And if you ever come to your senses about that little blonde piano player, I'll be around."

Alice watched her collect her things and leave. She was still confused and angry several hours later as she made her way to another appointment.

Between business meetings with her father in Dallas at least twice a week, a kitchen fire at one of her restaurants in Laredo, and a steady stream of Hot Check fans hanging around the parking lot of their condo, Alice felt as though she and Ricky would never have any privacy again. And to further complicate matters, Ricky was coming down with a cold.

"I'm such a whiny bitch when I'm sick," Ricky said as she put the finishing touches on their Saturday morning omelets.

Alice liked the domestic part of their busy lives. Moments snatched here and there were very special. They'd worked out a routine that seemed to revolve around food. Quality time consisted of having lunch together whenever possible. Ricky's writing schedule was flexible, but occasionally when she was really onto something a lunch date wasn't practical. Dinner, however, had become an evening ritual. If Alice had to work late, Ricky picked something up for a feast at the office. A few hours here and there before one of them had to be somewhere seemed to be working. They were both on the road a lot, usually in different directions, but under Alice's watchful eye they had a semblance of order to their lives.

A few days later Alice woke up to a blaring alarm clock and an empty bed. She found her robe hanging on the back of the bathroom door and slipped it around her nude body before going to search for Ricky. A lamp was on in the living room, and the smell of fresh coffee made her shuffle to the kitchen a little faster. She set the glass of orange juice on a small table and opened the door to Ricky's studio. Alice found her there working, dressed in pale yellow sweats and Reeboks. Ricky had headphones on and stopped occasionally only to scribble something down. She hadn't been to bed yet.

Ricky smiled and slipped off the headphones when she saw Alice. She took the orange juice Alice handed to her and enjoyed a healthy swallow.

"How's it going in here?" Alice asked. She sat on a stool beside her and glanced at the penciled notes on the sheet of music paper.

"Good."

"Can I hear it?"

"Sure." Ricky unplugged the headphones and turned a few knobs. Her fingers moved over the keys and produced a slow, bluesy strain.

Ricky never stopped surprising her. Every day was filled with something new to learn and appreciate. Alice had fallen hard for the stage persona that first night at Muldoon's, but there was more to this energetic singer than an incredible voice and those blue eyes that could see right into Alice's very soul. Ricky was a shy, modest genius, a passionate, sensitive friend, and a generous, caring lover. She was everything Alice had always wanted.

Ricky stopped playing and switched off the keyboard. "I'm eager to hear what Stan comes up with later on his bass." She took Alice's cup from her and set it on an amplifier close by. Their eyes met, and Ricky reached over and tugged the sash on Alice's robe. "Come here," she whispered.

Alice sat in her lap, straddling Ricky's thighs. Her robe hung loose, exposing her warm, nude body.

"Did watching me play get you all worked up?" Ricky asked. The tip of her tongue touched a firm, warm quivering nipple.

"I should've never told you that," Alice said. She rubbed her cheek against Ricky's soft hair and then laughed.

"It's not true?" Ricky asked.

"Yes, it's true, but that doesn't mean you have to bring it up all the time."

"I like thinking about it," Ricky said. She kissed her way up Alice's breast and found her eager, hungry mouth. Alice could hear herself purring as she gently took Ricky's bottom lip in between her teeth.

"I like thinking about it too," Alice whispered.

Ricky unpacked the Chinese food cartons and set them on the corner of Alice's desk. She hadn't been up very long and her voice still had the rough edges of sleep clinging to it.

"I'm sorry I'm late. Some kids were waiting for me at my car when I left home." She moved her chair closer to accommodate their usual eating arrangement in Alice's office.

Alice frowned. They couldn't go out anywhere lately without autograph seekers hounding them. Another *Rolling Stone* blurb had come out a few weeks ago and helped elevate the band to a new level of minicelebrity status. Joe was negotiating an offer as an opening act in the fall.

After a while, Alice folded her napkin and set it beside an empty shrimp-fried-rice carton. "Maybe we should start looking for a house," she said. "We need more room and a place where you can work. Something big enough for you and the boys to rehearse and record in, maybe." Alice watched Ricky nibble at a piece of shrimp tempura as the plan began to come together in her head. "Well? What do you think?"

"We'd be renting or buying?" Ricky asked, her voice dropping syllables in its huskiness.

"Buying, I think."

Ricky smiled. "A house with big trees and flowers. And two plastic pink flamingos in the front yard."

Alice went around her desk and reached for Ricky's hand to pull her up out of the chair. They rarely touched this way at the office, but Alice had to hold her now.

"A security fence, burglar bars, and a silent alarm," Alice said. She kissed her on the forehead and reveled in the strawberry scent of shampoo and soap. "But we can do the pink-flamingos-in-the-front-yard thing if you like."

Chapter Nine

Alice was summoned to Dallas again, and this time she didn't like the sound of it. Her father had been secretive about why he wanted her. She knew how much he enjoyed having people jump whenever he snapped his fingers, and it annoyed her when she was expected to jump as high as everyone else.

In her mind she went over the quarterly reports for her division and knew everything was going well there. Profits were up, thanks to another Ricky Conrad jingle, so she wasn't worried about any of that. She was ready for him.

He managed to surprise her, though, once she was seated in his office and heard that she was to handle the merger in New Orleans. Alice felt certain that her blood pressure had zoomed off the charts. She took the stack of papers her father gave her and prayed that he didn't notice her hand shaking.

"Look these over," he said. "Scott Briscoe is representing us, of course, and will be going with you. Finalizing everything may take a week. Maybe longer."

Charles Collins came around the side of his desk and sat on its corner. He was tall and husky, and kept his silver hair cut short. He had a small gap between his two front teeth and seldom smiled because of it. His gray suit looked new, just like everything else he owned. Alice had caught the scent of Old Spice when she hugged him. He'd worn it as long as she could remember.

"You've done an excellent job on the restaurants, Alice. You were able to take a neglected, struggling chain and make it appealing and profitable. But," he said as he put his hands together, "it's time for you to move on. Once this merger is complete, I want you to take over the New Orleans operation. Staffing, stocking, and inventory. Build it up. The market for tourism was virtually unexplored by the previous owner. One store in particular is near the French Quarter, but nothing's been done to capitalize on the tourist potential. Look into these things. Each store has its own personality. You'll have complete control and a generous budget. I know you can make it work."

Alice adjusted the folds of her long skirt and held the papers in trembling hands. "I don't know what to say," she whispered. Her mind was racing with details, but she was unable to put them into words just yet. The idea he was suggesting threw her into a panic. It meant an extended separation from Ricky.

"You'll be getting a substantial raise," he continued, "and a vast amount of experience. If I remember correctly, you started out here in retail after college. This will be a little different. Any problems you have, feel free to give me a call."

Not on your life, she thought with a sardonic laugh. A call to her father would only mean a sign of weakness to him. *Any problems that come up I either handle myself or die trying.*

"If all goes well in New Orleans," he said once he was behind his desk again, "I'll be retiring in the next year. Your mother and I want to travel while we're still young enough to enjoy it. Frankly, Alice, I believe you're ready to take over the company now, but I feel like the more experience I can give you, the better equipped you'll be when the time comes." His huge leather chair squeaked as he leaned back in it. He was comfortable in his role. The king teasing the princess with talk of abdication. "You also need to select your replacement for the South Texas area. I have a few names for you if you can't find someone suitable." He laughed suddenly, as if seeing her for the first time. "You're pale. Are you all right?"

"I guess I'm a little overwhelmed," she said. Not only was he shipping her off to New Orleans, but in a year she'd be running the entire company! *Am I ready for that? Jesus!*

"I'm not throwing you entirely to the wolves," he said. "Scott will be there to help you on legal matters and such. You have office space downtown and a condo for you — and also one for your secretary if she decides to go with you. If not, you can make arrangements for your replacement to keep her on. A competent and resourceful secretary is something I couldn't do without. I hope you can convince her to go with you."

"She has children and family in San Antonio. I'm not sure she'll want to move," Alice said calmly. On the outside she was a tower of strength, but inside she was beginning to crumble. "So the merger should take a week," she said slowly, sorting it out in her mind as she went, "and then I'm in New Orleans getting the stores together."

"Right. Any problem?"

"No," she said. "My replacement won't be worth much for a few weeks. I'll probably have to juggle both jobs."

He nodded. "You may want to keep that in mind when you select someone. By the way, your mother expects you for dinner this evening."

Alice stood up and put the papers he'd given her in her briefcase. She glanced at her watch and shook her head. "I really can't stay. There's so much to do. I'll stop by and see her on my way to the airport."

During the flight back Alice went over the papers and familiarized herself with figures and names. She buried herself in retail lingo and tried not to think about how Ricky would take the news. A week in New Orleans on the merger was one thing, but a transfer was something else altogether.

It was nearly eight when she got home. The band

was playing at a club in Austin and wouldn't be back until around three-thirty that morning. Alice called her secretary at home, wanting to give her as much notice about the New Orleans deal as she could. Hopefully Gloria would be willing to transfer with her. They'd worked together for years, and the prospect of having an office without Gloria was almost as traumatic as having to move to another state without Ricky.

She sat in the dark with the stereo on low and finished a glass of wine. Alice tried to think of a way to break the news to Ricky, but nothing creative was coming to her. They were looking at no less than a year apart, maybe longer if her father didn't retire. *A promotion shouldn't be this damned complicated!*

Alice was asleep on the sofa when Ricky finally came home. Ricky knelt beside her and gave her a little shake. "Wake up, baby," she said gently. "Let's go to bed."

Alice stretched and put her arms around Ricky's neck, filling her hands with that soft, thick hair. She found Ricky's mouth and kissed her with deep, probing urgency. Alice felt a surge of heat beginning to pulsate between her legs as Ricky burrowed into her neck. Alice tilted her head and encouraged her to continue with a whimper.

"I didn't expect you back so soon," Ricky said into her ear. She sucked on Alice's earlobe and then said, "How'd it go?"

Alice pulled her down and whispered, "We'll talk about it later." She tugged Ricky's T-shirt over her head and found her mouth again. "Come here."

Clothing fell to the floor and became wadded up beneath them during a new wave of excitement. After fumbling with shirt buttons and muddling through several hasty attempts at bra removal, Ricky freed Alice's breasts and rubbed her own into them. The tip of her tongue touched just below Alice's ear before she ran her fingernails gently down her ribs. Alice managed to get her knee between Ricky's legs and lifted it to find a welcome wet reception.

Ricky made the most wonderful sounds, the throaty gasps, the husky moans, and listening to them was rewarding to Alice. Ricky began to move against her in a slow, steady motion, and Alice closed her eyes and tilted her head back again as Ricky's lips met hers. Every cell in Alice's body was fully awake with want and anticipation. She loved having Ricky this way — fresh from the club with the smoke still clinging to her body. Ricky kissed Alice's shoulder and worked up to the crook of her neck while her hair played against Alice's skin.

Simply listening to Ricky and feeling her move made Alice ready to come. She grabbed Ricky's head and found her mouth again, searching and sucking on her tongue as her fingers wound through Ricky's hair and fondled it shamelessly. Alice could never get enough of its silky texture. She loved touching it, loved smelling it, loved feeling it on her skin.

"It's good," Alice said, her voice no more than an urgent whisper. "So good."

Their usual approach to sex almost always involved Ricky making love to Alice first, which was then followed by a more leisurely, relaxed version of their mutual desire for each other. Alice could be ready for her with no more than a suggestive look or a heated kiss, but it usually took more for Ricky. Alice lived for those moments when Ricky became sexually vulnerable, and tonight was promising to be one of those times.

Alice spread her legs a little and slipped her hand down between them, touching herself and matching Ricky's rocking motion. Alice had never particularly cared for masturbation until she realized how much Ricky liked watching her. They didn't make love this way often, but it was always so hot when they did.

Alice opened herself with her fingers and dipped into warm creamy folds. The moment Ricky realized what she was doing, her breathing changed, and the grinding became more desperate and primitive. There was a long raspy groan that caused a sudden return of that roller-coaster feeling in Alice's stomach. Ricky buried her face in Alice's neck and came with a shudder. She covered Alice's face with tiny erratic kisses as she rubbed herself slowly against Alice's wet thigh.

"You make it so easy," Ricky whispered. She kissed her, and Alice felt the tumbling start all over again. Ricky's mouth moved down Alice's body, stopping only long enough to savor each breast before easing farther down. Alice held herself open once more, spreading her legs and squirming with need as she waited for Ricky's mouth to touch her.

"Oh, yes . . ." Alice's senses came alive, and her desire soared as Ricky's tongue licked and probed with compelling accuracy. Alice put her hands on the back of Ricky's head and raised her hips in a primal display of urgency. Moaning, low and emphatic, filled the room, and a delirious surge of pleasure roared through Alice's body. She came hard and cried out Ricky's name as she thrashed on the sofa. Ricky worked her nose into Alice's wet, quivering center and slowly rubbed it up and down. She kissed her there tenderly and then kissed the inside of Alice's thigh over and over again.

Much later they lay on the sofa facing each other, dozing with legs entwined, naked except for one of Ricky's socks only halfway on. Alice touched Ricky's hair again, still finding it hard to keep her hands off of her.

"How was Austin?"

"Good," Ricky said with a yawn. "A rowdy crowd. My dad and Sharon were there for a while. Things are getting better between us." She kissed the corner of Alice's mouth. "How was Dallas? Did your father ask about me?"

Alice hugged her; the lump in her throat was there before she knew it. The transfer, the new job, the move, the necessity to live alone for a year without . . . Alice hugged Ricky again and brushed her cheek against her soft hair.

"Let's go to bed," she whispered. "I have to be up in three hours."

At the office the next day Alice made a list of possible replacements for her position and had Gloria set up interviews. She also got in touch with the company's lawyer and had a conference call with him on the merger. He would meet her in New Orleans in three days to go over a few other details, and they anticipated closing the deal by Wednesday at the latest.

"All next week you should be tied up with the current management and personnel," Scott said. He had been her father's lawyer since Alice was a little girl. "The stores will stay operational during the changeover, so you'll be hitting the ground running."

"And Wednesday after we close, I'm on my own," she said. Alice's replacement in South Texas wouldn't have much time to learn the ropes either, so basically, as she suspected, she would be working both jobs for a while. Alice saw herself being spread thinner and thinner as each phone call came in.

"Absolutely. I can be reached for any legal matters that come up, of course," Scott said.

Alice leaned back in her chair and rubbed her eyes. She glanced out her office window where the city of San Antonio seemed to be thumbing its nose at her. "How many people expect me to fall on my face, Scott?"

"Your father has all the confidence in the world in you. His opinion is the one that counts, I'd say."

"That many, huh?"

Chapter Ten

She made sure Ricky could be home at a decent
hour and picked up enough pizza for everyone. The
band was going over some new material Ricky had
been working on.

Alice could hear them when she came in. She set
her briefcase next to the sofa and balanced the three
large pizzas with her other hand. The boxes were
still surprisingly warm as she set them down on the
table. She opened the door to the music room and
waved at Kyle who was reading a magazine. The
other three didn't hear her come in.

Ricky stopped playing and motioned for Joe and Stan to stop also. "We'll need a rim shot here," she said, pointing at Kyle, "then you've got a brief solo after the third verse. That's what I'm hearing in my head now, but feel free to change my mind later."

"How long before we have lyrics on this one?" Joe asked. He played a lick on his guitar and then noticed Alice leaning against the doorjamb. "Yo, Ricky. Your woman's here."

Alice smiled. "And her woman brought pizza," she said.

Guitars came off and the magazine closed. Rehearsal was officially over.

The five of them sat around the dining room table laughing and eating. The boys drank beer while Ricky and Alice shared a tumbler of orange juice.

"Did she tell you who called today?" Stan asked Alice. His eyes lit up, and from all angles across the table, Joe, Stan and Kyle stretched for a high five.

Not waiting for Alice to answer, Stan blurted, "Doug Cooper! Called right here on your phone!" He rummaged through the pizza box and came out with a huge limp slice.

"Doug Cooper the singer?" Alice said. "The 'Say It Ain't So' Doug Cooper?"

"Jesus," Kyle mumbled. "Even Alice knows who he is! He must really be hot shit."

"Number one album for five weeks in a row and number one song for three," Alice said.

Ricky's laughter brought them all out of a stunned shock.

"How did you know that?" Joe asked with a dab of suspicion in his voice.

"You mean she's right?" Stan said. His eyes were wide with surprise. Everyone had stopped eating.

"*Rolling Stone*," Alice said. "I read every word of it when it comes in. There's a great article on the Dynamos, by the way. Have you seen it?"

Ricky snickered and laughed heartily at the expression on Joe's face.

"Why would Doug Cooper call here?" Alice asked. "And how did he get our telephone number?"

"He wants Ricky to sing a duet with him," Stan said. The boys reached across the table for another high five.

Alice looked at Ricky, who was still nibbling on the same piece of pizza she'd started with ten minutes ago. "That's wonderful," Alice said.

"Try to convince *her* of that," Stan grumbled.

"What did he say? Did he call you personally?"

Ricky shrugged. "His agent got my number from the guy who produced our last album. Doug knows what he wants, but I'm sure I'm not the only female singer he's talking to. Besides, I'm not interested in recording with anyone else."

"It's a duet," Stan said. "It's not like real music. This could be good for all of us. Hot Check too."

"Yeah, maybe," Ricky said.

"Who's got the number two song?" Joe asked Alice. His squinty eyes looked as though they were hoping to spring a trick question on her.

"The Crooners," Alice said with a smirk. "Up from number three."

"Damn," Joe mumbled, and then shook his head. He laughed after a moment. "Damn."

"Why ya gotta be so negative all the time, Ricky?" Stan whined. "Doug Cooper wants you. Let's enjoy that concept for a while. Maybe he's smarter than we're giving him credit for. Just because his music sucks doesn't mean he's stupid, you know. Trying to get you on one of his albums is a fucking flash of brilliance on *somebody*'s part."

Kyle reached for another slice of pizza and nodded toward Stan. "Where'd you find this guy?"

Three empty pizza boxes and a six-pack later the boys were gone and Alice and Ricky were alone. "They can put away some serious pizza," Ricky said, her gravelly voice taking on a soft tone. She stacked the boxes and piled napkins and empty beer cans on top. "They eat like every meal's their last."

Alice followed her into the kitchen and set the dirty plates on the counter. She straightened her skirt and leaned against the sink. It had been a nice, relaxed evening, and Alice didn't like ruining it, but she wanted to get this over with.

"I'm being transferred," she said, the words nearly sticking in her throat. It was so quiet that she could hear them both breathing.

"You're what?"

"I'm being transferred to New Orleans." She crossed her arms over her chest. "I didn't know how to tell you."

"What's in New Orleans? Aren't all of your restaurants here in Texas?"

"It's a new job. Retail. Department store management."

Ricky shook the hair out of her eyes with a little toss of her head. "Have you already made up your mind to take it? Without even discussing it with me?"

"There's no room for discussion where my father's concerned."

"So when is all of this supposed to happen?"

The lump was back in her throat almost immediately. "Saturday," Alice said. "I'm coordinating the merger beginning on Saturday."

Ricky's voice had been gradually growing louder. She backed up against the sink and put her hands on the counter behind her. "You're leaving me in three *days*? Jesus, Alice. Have you thought about any of this?"

"I'm not leaving you. After the merger when things settle down a little, I'll be able to come back on weekends."

"Weekends? I *work* weekends!" Ricky was out of the kitchen and charging through the apartment.

"When you're off during the week you can fly to New Orleans," Alice said as she followed her. "I don't like this any better than you do, but I have other responsibilities, Ricky."

"Great. What about us? Whose responsibility is that?" Ricky looked at her with blue eyes swimming in tears. "Jesus. I don't believe this. You're leaving me for a *job*? I can't go through this again."

"I'm not *leaving* you!" Alice caught that familiar gleam of rebellion in those blue eyes, that same glimpse that had attracted her to Ricky the first night they met. "My work is very important to me. This merger and this transfer mean everything to my career, Ricky. When somebody gives you a promotion, you don't say no!"

"You're throwing away what we have for a goddamn pat on the head from your father!" Ricky yelled. "What did he do this time, Alice? Give you another raise? Promise to leave you everything? Jesus, you make more money *now* than we could ever spend!" She whirled around and headed for the door. "If you leave me, it's over."

"This is crazy!" Alice scrambled toward the door after her. "You're upset. You don't know what you're saying. We *love* each other, goddamn it!" Alice grabbed her and pressed her body into Ricky's, pinning her against the door in order to keep her from leaving. They were looking right at each other, their bodies warm, their breasts touching, their faces only inches apart. Alice could see the fear in Ricky's eyes, and couldn't believe how much she wanted her right then.

"The difference in us seems to be that I'm in love with you," Ricky said slowly, "and you're in love with your goddamn career."

Alice released her and stepped back, stunned by her words. "You never fight fair," Alice said, sounding more in control than she felt. "Never."

Ricky yanked the door open. "The truth hurts, doesn't it?"

"Ricky," she said shakily. "We can work this out. Will you listen to yourself? You're saying that you'd rather settle for nothing. Is that what you want?" The thought of losing her had never occurred to Alice before. *Why is she being so unreasonable? So unwilling to compromise?* "Where are you going?" Alice demanded once she realized that Ricky was out in the hallway already.

"Hell, I don't know," she said. She looked lost and hurt, as if her only friend in the world had just tossed her out in the street. All Alice wanted to do was hold her and make it better.

"I love you, Alice. I've never loved anyone the way I love you." Her voice was nearly gone as she held onto the door. "I can't believe this is happening all over again. When Emily left me she said it was for a two-week vacation. And she never came back."

"I'm not Emily," Alice whispered, resenting the comparison. She reached for Ricky's hand and slowly coaxed her back inside the apartment. She took her into her arms and kissed the top of her head. "I'm not Emily."

Ricky searched Alice's face once more, and closed her eyes. "I know who you are," she said in her ragged voice, "and it's not helping much right now."

The next day Alice selected her replacement and relayed her choice to her father. Once she took time to think about it, she knew who would be right for her job. The interviews were more or less a formality.

All day long Alice had considered the merger, the changes needed in the takeover, and the awesome responsibility her father had given her. She had confidence in her abilities and was glad that he had that kind of confidence in her as well, but there were people at Collins Enterprises that Alice still had to prove herself to. Several associates saw her as a fortunate but unprepared answer to their corporate future.

The following afternoon Joe came by to see her. His attire was a bit more conservative than his usual blue jeans and T-shirt. He wore black pants, a crisp white shirt, shined black boots, and a black bolo tie. Alice smiled when she saw him, remembering a remark Ricky had made once about how presentable the boys could be when you cleaned them up a little. It seemed like another lifetime ago when Joe Langley had first sat in that same chair discussing Alice's jingle and Ricky Conrad's talent.

"What's the occasion?" she asked.

"Something's going on with Ricky, and I was hoping you'd tell me what it is."

Alice drummed neatly trimmed nails on the edge of her desk. He deserved to know what was happening, and she was surprised that Ricky hadn't told him already. "I'm being transferred to New Orleans almost immediately, and we're both upset about it," Alice said.

Joe swore under his breath, but Alice didn't quite catch the exact string of expletives. He looked at her and slowly shook his head. "So what are you doing about it? Ricky doesn't work well when she's upset. Her voice has been rough from crying for two days."

"We're working on it."

"Are you two breaking up?" he asked. His dark eyes were huge and accusing. "You can't do this to me, Alice. Goddamn it. You can't do this."

"What am I doing to you?"

"You're bailing out, aren't you? Jesus! She's fucking in *love* with you!"

"Lower your voice," Alice said calmly. "Listen to

me, Joe. If you'd like to help, then fix her schedule so she gets a few days off during the week. I'll be back on weekends. We'll see each other as often as possible by flying back and forth."

Joe leaned forward in his chair, dark eyes narrow and menacing. "Are you dumping her?"

"Of course not! How can you even suggest such a thing?"

"If you're not bailing out, then why haven't you asked me to move the band again?"

Alice blinked several times in confusion. *Move the band again. Move the band to New Orleans.* Alice's heart skipped a beat once the suggestion began to sink in.

"I mean, it's the jazz capital of the world and all," he said, "but there's gotta be a market for some rock 'n' roll there somewhere. I'd have to check it out, of course." He stopped and raked his hand through the top of his long black hair. "But we're not moving anywhere if this is your way of getting out of this thing with Ricky. I need some honesty here, Alice. Don't bullshit me."

Alice closed her eyes and let out a frustrated groan of her own. She rubbed the bridge of her nose and could feel another headache on its way.

"If you can get the band relocated to New Orleans," she said in a controlled, quiet voice, "Ricky and I will be eternally grateful to you."

Joe nodded and then sprang out of his chair. "Just don't lie to me, okay?"

They looked at each other in an uncomfortable silence, each very aware of how important the other was in Ricky's life.

"I'm in love with her too, you know," Alice said simply.

Joe nodded again and stuck his hands in his pockets. "You goddamn well better be."

Saturday morning Alice was packed and ready to go. Ricky hadn't been to bed yet since they'd stayed up talking and making love after Ricky got home from the club. Alice hoped to be able to get some sleep on the plane. She had a meeting with Scott Briscoe at two that afternoon.

"I left some phone numbers where you can reach me," Alice said. "The merger should be wrapped up by Wednesday. Hopefully I'll be home Friday night for the weekend."

Ricky squeezed Alice's hand as she maneuvered the Jaguar in and out of traffic. "I've been whining, haven't I?"

Alice laughed softly. "You deserve to whine a little."

"I'm sorry I've been such a baby about this. I said some terrible things to you the other night." She let go of Alice's hand and gripped the steering wheel.

"Let's just hope Joe comes through and finds something permanent for the band in New Orleans."

They made small talk while they waited for passengers to board. Alice wanted to keep her talking so Ricky wouldn't cry. She had to work that night, and it would take most of the day to get her voice back.

"What's your schedule like this week?" Alice asked.

"Recording and rehearsing. The usual. I think Joe's got us booked in Corpus for a party or a fund-raiser on Thursday. I'm not sure which. He promised to fix the schedule the week after, though. Maybe you and I can fly back together on Sunday."

As passengers began to board, Ricky hugged her. "Don't send me any postcards, okay?" she whispered into Alice's ear. "And try to be agreeable at this merger thing. Don't be a hard ass and give them an excuse to keep you over the weekend."

Alice laughed and kissed her lightly on the lips. "I won't. I'll call you when I get there."

Alice settled into her condo near downtown New Orleans and went over the contracts Scott Briscoe had given her earlier. They were meeting with the current owner's lawyers in the morning; Scott had briefed her thoroughly.

"You've done your homework," he said to her over a late lunch Sunday afternoon. He was in his mid-fifties with bushy gray hair and a thin Errol Flynn mustache.

She had tried most of the day to get in touch with Ricky, but there had been no answer at home or the boys' place. Alice finally got through to her early Monday morning and was relieved to finally hear that gravelly, sleep-filled voice.

"Good morning," Alice said.

"Good morning," came the sleepy croak in return. "I miss you already."

"I miss you too."

"What's on your agenda today?" Ricky asked.

117

Alice sighed. "Imagine a room full of bickering, cigar-smoking lawyers arguing over inventory and stock prices."

"Makes a day with the boys sound pretty good."

"Go back to sleep, baby," Alice said softly. "Call me when you get home tonight."

Alice got a break from negotiations on Thursday afternoon and talked to her secretary, Gloria, on the phone. Together they solved what problems they could, and the rest Alice would have to take care of when she got back. Gloria knew enough about what was going on at the office in San Antonio to handle the routine things that came up, but with Alice's replacement still trying to get settled in, there really wasn't anyone actually "in charge" yet. Gloria wouldn't be following her to New Orleans for several more weeks yet. The San Antonio office needed her there much worse than Alice needed her in New Orleans at the moment.

Alice got held up in a meeting until after eleven Thursday evening. Everyone was working hard to get the thing reconciled and merged properly, but it was looking more and more like they would be stuck there working over the weekend. By the time she got back to her condo, Alice was exhausted. She tried to call Ricky at home, but got no answer. She went to bed, knowing that Ricky would call her when she got in later.

Chapter Eleven

It was four-thirty the next morning before Alice was finally jarred awake by the telephone. She squinted at the clock and reached for the receiver. "Hello," she said.

"Alice? This is Henry Conrad. Ricky's been in an accident."

Alice didn't remember getting dressed or driving herself to the airport. She caught a flight out of New Orleans and spent the entire trip in a daze, too stunned to do anything but tremble. Kyle picked her up at the San Antonio airport. He didn't seem to be

119

functioning well either. They were both in shock and stood helplessly saying nothing. He opened his arms just as Alice stepped into them — Kyle needed to hold someone as much as Alice needed to be held. He hugged her and wiped his eyes on the sleeve of his T-shirt.

"She's got a concussion," he said quietly. "There's no fracture, but she hasn't come out of it yet."

On the way to the hospital, he told her that Stan had been driving and swerved to miss a deer. The car rolled and Stan had been thrown out and killed instantly.

"Joe fucked his hand up getting to Ricky," he said, his voice breaking. "We think she was asleep when it happened. She had a headache earlier." He sniffed and then cleared his throat. "We were behind them and watched it all happen. It didn't seem real. None of it. When we reached them we could smell the gas everywhere, and somebody started yelling about a fire. We couldn't get the fucking *door* open so we smashed a window." He was crying openly now, and Alice felt the first rush of tears fill her eyes. She hadn't been able to cry before this, and now she wasn't sure she'd ever be able to stop.

"I can't believe he's dead," Kyle whispered. "I still can't believe it. None of it makes any fucking sense."

At the hospital Alice found Henry Conrad, his wife Sharon, and Joe sitting in the waiting area of the intensive care unit. Alice felt nauseated and detached, as if someone else were in her body making her do the things that were expected of her. She could see everything that was going on but had trouble relating to any of it. She felt as though she were walking under water.

Alice noticed Joe's heavily bandaged left arm, which was snug in a sling close to his chest. She sat down beside him and reached over to take his other hand.

"Why is this happening, Alice?" he whispered, squeezing her hand as though his life depended on it.

Alice looked straight ahead, not seeing anything. She felt so removed from it all, as if it were happening to someone else.

"Stan's dead," he whispered. "He's dead. Ricky has to come out of this. She has to."

The words beaded up and rolled off as if Scotchgard had been sprayed on her.

"She was like a rag doll when I picked her up," Joe said. A sob caught in his throat, and he tilted his head back and closed his eyes. "I keep looking for Stan everywhere. He should be here waiting with us."

Alice nodded and unsuccessfully blinked back tears. "I know," she said. They were the first words she'd spoken since picking up her plane ticket hours ago. "I'm looking for him too."

When the doctor, a short plump middle-aged man, finally came out, he directed all information to them as a group. He said that Ricky had a bruise and that he had no idea when she would regain consciousness. They'd run several tests and were giving her medication to reduce fluids. Two visitors per hour, on the hour, were allowed in to see her.

Alice turned away from all of them, the shock still thrashing her around like a cork in a churning sea.

Since Henry and Sharon had seen her several times already, when the hour came around it was decided that Alice and Joe would go in to see her. They moved down the hall, purposeful in their strides, not wanting to waste any of their rationed time. They passed through swinging doors into a totally white environment, but nothing could have prepared them for what they saw.

The room had several occupied beds in a semi-circle and a nurse's station in the center. There was an eerie sort of quiet even though the insistent beeping of life-support machines seemed to be everywhere. No moaning or conscious patients. Alice had the feeling that the room itself was responsible for Ricky's condition. If she could just take her out of there, everything might be all right again.

Alice and Joe stood by Ricky's bed staring at the tubes and other gadgets hooked up to her. She had a large goose egg-shaped bump on the right side of her head, a terrible looking black eye, and several dark bruises on her arms. Alice reached up, her hand shaking badly, and touched Ricky's cheek. Joe put his arm around Alice's shoulder as she leaned against him gratefully.

"My God," she whispered, the tears stinging her eyes.

"She looks so small," Alice heard him say in a tone full of wonder.

Alice touched a huge bruise on Ricky's arm and

felt a lurching in her stomach. She wasn't sure if she would be sick or not. She swallowed several times and blinked back more tears.

"Your time's up," the nurse said.

Alice didn't even remember being led out of the room.

Alice offered the condo to Henry and Sharon so they could get some sleep and grab a shower, but Alice wouldn't leave the hospital. She stayed and waited for any sign of a change; she didn't want to take the chance of missing anything. Sharon brought her something to eat, but Alice wasn't hungry.

"You need some sleep, Alice," she said. "I'll call you if there's anything new."

"I'm fine." The tears flowed so easily that she didn't even know when they started.

Alice didn't really begin to come out of shock until she saw her secretary among the group of people in the waiting room the next morning. That stern, serious face and her red flyaway hair was a welcome sight. Gloria made her way through the crowd and gave Alice a hug for moral support.

"How is she?"

"The same," Alice whispered. She had no strength to speak any louder.

"You look terrible."

"I don't doubt that for a moment."

"I know this is a bad time," Gloria said awkwardly, "but Mr. Briscoe needs for you to call him at once."

Alice looked at her quickly. "The merger," she said. "I'd forgotten all about it! Christ!"

Scott was furious when Alice finally got him on the telephone. He ranted, raved, and attacked her competency to handle such a large responsibility, but Alice was in no mood to be preached at by anyone.

"Merge without me," she said. "You need me there only to sign the final papers. Are they any closer to doing that?"

"Yes," he barked. "Tomorrow."

"Call my secretary when they're ready. I'll fly down and sign them. I expect you to earn your money, Scott. And I'd appreciate it if my absence didn't get back to my father. Do you understand what I'm saying?" Her tone of voice registered quickly with him, and he didn't say anything else. "I wouldn't be here if this weren't an emergency."

"I'm sorry about all of that, Alice, but let me stress once again how important it is that you be here. You're representing Collins Enterprises. You're representing your father."

"I know exactly who I'm representing, Scott. I'll be there when you've done all you can do, and not a minute before."

She hung up and rested her head against the phone. She needed to make a quick appearance in New Orleans for a few days during the week to sign the papers and get a feel for how things were going, but there was no way she could go back yet. At least not until Ricky's condition improved. Once Alice stopped to think about it, she realized that she should tell her father what was going on, but she had no desire to talk to him at this point. She didn't want to talk to anyone but the doctor.

* * * * *

Stan's funeral was the next day, and hundreds of
people were there to pay their respects. Joe held
Alice's hand through the eulogy, squeezing it tightly
ever so often. His left arm was still heavily bandaged
and tucked close to his body.

Everyone who stopped to express their condolences
asked about Ricky. Alice knew very few of the people,
but everyone seemed to know her. She found it
strange that Ricky should have so many friends that
she knew nothing about. At times their life together
had excluded almost everyone else. *That will have to
change*, Alice decided. *I should know these people.*

Kyle drove to the cemetery with Joe and Alice in
the front seat. No one spoke. After the funeral the
three of them went back to the hospital to wait on
word from the doctor.

Henry and Sharon went in to see Ricky that
evening and came out with good news. She had come
to briefly, but then was back out again. They had
run more tests on her earlier and the results looked
better. There were smiles and hugs everywhere.

Dora came by with a McDonald's bag full of
treats and did her best to try to pump some life back
into Alice.

"You've gotta eat," Dora argued. "You look
terrible. What good will you be to her if you don't
take care of yourself?"

Later that evening Henry and Alice went in to
see her. The nurse on duty informed them that Ricky

was awake. Alice felt her heart flutter and fresh tears flood her eyes at the news, but again, neither of them were ready for what they saw.

Ricky's eyes were open, but she acted as though she couldn't see anything — as if neither of her visitors were there. The bruises on her arms were darker, and she looked awful.

"Go ahead and talk to her," the nurse said. "She can hear you."

"Why is she so spacey?" Henry asked. "Can't she see us?"

"She'll be slow for days. Sleep is the best thing for her now."

"Ricky," Alice whispered. Ricky gave her a blank stare and then pulled at the sheet before going back to sleep.

Renewed shock began to take hold of her as they stood there watching and waiting. *She's getting better,* Alice thought. *They say she's getting better.*

The next day Ricky was moved to a private room where all she did was sleep. Alice, Henry, and Sharon stayed with her during the day, but Alice was with her alone in the evening. Visitors were always in and out of the room, and the telephone rang constantly.

Joe came by early one evening after a swarm of visitors had just left.

"Kyle's gone," he said. There was a resignation in his voice that worried Alice for a moment. "No one knows where he went. Packed his stuff up last night."

Alice felt queasy. *Stan's dead, Ricky's in the*

hospital and Kyle's gone. She studied Joe's thin, somber face. He seemed smaller now and somewhat wilted around the edges.

"How's your arm?" she asked him. The bandage was white and fresh, extending from fingertips to just past the elbow.

"A guitar player with severed tendons," he said. "I've got nothing but unemployment in my future."

Alice took a slow, deep breath. Her eyes met his in a moment of strained silence. "Please tell me you're joking."

"No, Alice," he said simply, "it's no joke. I'll probably never play another lick as long as I live. Ricky's got some serious shit to deal with when she wakes up." His face paled, and his right hand began to shake. "We had everything. We were on our way." He stopped talking and seemed to wilt again, as if someone had let all the air out of him. His eyes darted to the bed where Ricky lay in an unnatural sleep. A calm seemed to come over him as he watched her. "She's the best friend I ever had, Alice. I'd do anything for her. It seems like we've been together forever."

Alice nodded, knowing the feeling well. "I want you to see another doctor tomorrow," she said. "Get another opinion. Have them send me the bill."

He shifted in the chair. "There's no feeling in my fingers. I know it's over for me." He looked at Ricky again. "She's very fragile, Alice. This is gonna be hard on her."

"I know," Alice whispered. "We'll help her."

Will this end? she wondered. *Will things ever be normal again?*

Chapter Twelve

Ironically the accident gave a tremendous boost to the band's new single, raising it seven notches into the Top Forty. Joe spent as much time on the phone as Alice did, canceling all of their engagements and turning down offers.

Alice pulled herself together long enough to fly back to New Orleans and briefly meet with her new staff. She had scores of employees wondering whether or not they all still had jobs. Even with the responsibility of the south Texas restaurants to deal with in addition to the merger in Louisiana, the old Alice was slowly beginning to resurface.

She called Ricky's room every few hours to talk to either Joe, Henry, or Sharon about any progress Ricky had made, but the report was always the same. Ricky slept constantly, and when she did wake up she seemed too out of it to know anything.

Alice flew back to San Antonio with a briefcase full of personnel files. She was able to stay in Ricky's room with her throughout the night and managed to get most of her work done once all the visitors were gone.

The following morning Alice's father called the hospital from Dallas and inquired about Ricky's condition. Alice explained that she was doing much better. She didn't ask how he found out about the accident and didn't really want to know even though he seemed annoyed that she hadn't told him sooner. Her life with Ricky was something Alice wanted to keep separate from him. She liked to think of it as one of the few things he had no control over.

Alice was grateful that her father didn't try to pressure her into returning to New Orleans. He never even mentioned it. She sensed that he trusted her to handle things, and left it at that. It had been a social call, and she didn't get many of those.

"When they release her I'd like to take her home

with me," Henry said to Alice the next morning. "Sharon can be with her all day. Ricky'll need that."

"I don't think so," Alice said. "She belongs with me. I'll hire a nurse to stay with her."

"If you're staying here in town," Henry said, "then that's okay. But if you're thinking about taking her with you to New Orleans, then no way. The doctor won't let her travel that far yet."

"You've asked him about this already?" she snapped.

Alice eventually allowed herself to be persuaded by both Henry and the doctor to wait before making such a long trip, but the thought of Henry and his wife taking care of Ricky made Alice very uneasy. *She belongs with me*, she kept thinking over and over again. "You're not taking her to Austin with you."

"We'll wait until she's a little better first." Henry's tone was warm. "Sharon and I can take care of her here at your place."

Alice wasn't too thrilled about that either, but there wasn't much else she could do. Hopefully Ricky would recover faster in more familiar surroundings.

With all of that to worry about, Alice also received another phone call from her father, who had more plans for her already.

"I've registered you for a fashion merchandising seminar in New York next week," Mr. Collins said. "I'm sure you're fairly rusty in that area being as you've been tucked away in restaurant management for the last few years."

"I can't make it next week," Alice said. *You've got some lousy timing, Dad. Here I am only inches away from finally getting my lover back, and you want me to go to a goddamn seminar?*

"You'll have to make this one, Alice. There isn't another one for six months. I need you up on this." He was rigid and unyielding. She heard it in his voice. There would be a yes in her answer or else.

"How long is it?" she asked.

"It's only three days. Afterward I'll get with you on what I have in mind for New Orleans."

"You said I'd be running things," she reminded him. *How in the hell am I going to get out of this?*

"I'll only be pointing you in the right direction."

"I really don't want to go anywhere with Ricky's condition no better than this."

"We can't wait six months for another seminar of this caliber, Alice. You'll go to this one. Doesn't she have family? Other friends who can help her?"

"Things are complicated," she said, having no desire to get into this with him now. "Yes, of course, she has family. I guess she'll be fine." She said it as much for herself as for him. Yes, Sharon and Henry would take excellent care of Ricky, but Alice didn't want that. *I want to take care of her.* "Three days in New York," she said. "Jesus."

Henry helped Alice get Ricky in the car. They drove to the condo and put her to bed where she slept for five hours straight without ever moving. Sharon catered to her constantly, making her eat when she finally woke up, fluffing her pillows, keeping the television on programs she thought Ricky would like. Alice wanted to do those things for her, but eventually she felt more in the way than anything else.

"She never watches TV," Alice said.

"I know that, but what else does she have to do?" Sharon poured fresh cups of coffee and sat down with Alice at the table. "She's getting better. They said sleep was good for her."

Alice pushed her coffee away, tired of the caffeine that was keeping her up until all hours of the night. If only she could sleep it all away like Ricky was doing, everything would be so much easier.

"I have to make an appearance in New Orleans tomorrow," Alice said, "and then it looks like I may have to attend a seminar in New York. After that I'm coming to get her. She should be well enough to travel by then."

"What's she gonna do in New Orleans?" Sharon asked. Her green eyes danced with anger. "How will we know if she needs us?"

"There are telephones."

"You're gonna keep her cooped up in some penthouse all day?"

"I'll be with her."

"What about work?"

"I'll make arrangements. Look," Alice said gently, "I have to take care of her now. I *want* to take care of her now."

Sharon stirred her coffee and pushed her long dark hair away from her face. She looked at Alice thoughtfully for a moment and then shook her head. "She needs her family now."

"*I'm* her family!"

"It's not the same."

Alice sighed and gave in to the coffee, sipping it carefully. She refused to argue about this any more. She didn't have the energy.

* * * * *

Alice slept in a chair in their bedroom in case Ricky needed anything during the night. She was a small lump in the huge bed, and Alice was just so grateful to have her home again. Ricky slept like a rock, but Alice was nervous about being in the same bed with her just yet. Henry and Sharon had the guest room and were pretty much in the way and into everything.

When Ricky was awake, she offered little more than blank expressions, distant stares, and prompted responses to questions. She was able to give brief answers when asked something directly and seemed almost to recognize everyone who came to see her, even though she never said anything.

She treated Alice the same way she treated all of her visitors, with no acknowledgment that she was anything more than just a vaguely familiar face. Joe was there too, feeling as uncertain and out of place as Alice did. Alice found him sitting at the keyboard in Ricky's music room hitting keys with his right hand.

"How long is her old man staying?" he asked. "Doesn't he have to work or something?"

Alice offered a weak smile. Joe didn't care too much for Henry Conrad either these days. "He's back and forth almost as much as I am."

"I guess she's getting better," he said. "It's hard to tell."

"We'll have her back soon."

Alice caught an early flight to New Orleans the

133

next morning and felt a renewed uneasiness come over her. *Just how long will it take before the old Ricky is back?* she wondered.

Once in her new office, Alice immediately threw herself into her work. New job. New faces. New problems. She held meetings with her department heads and managers and was well aware of the resentment her youth could present to several of the older employees. She poured on the calm, sedate exterior and stuck to the straightforward approach, which effectively forestalled any trouble.

Alice got reports on Ricky over the phone every few hours or so while she was away. The merger was complete, and Alice was totally in charge and running on empty. Henry had mentioned earlier how Ricky's appetite had returned and how she even initiated conversation occasionally. Her marathon naps had become less frequent, and the blank stares were now only sporadic.

"I told her about Stan this morning," Henry said when Alice called that afternoon. "Joe's with her now."

"How'd she take it?"

"It's hard to say. She's so quiet."

"Does she understand what's going on?" Alice asked.

"She seems to."

Alice hung up and leaned her head back against her chair. *She's getting better, damn it. You'll have her here in another week.*

Whenever Alice called, Sharon claimed that Ricky

had just fallen asleep again. Alice continued asking questions until she got the answers she wanted. Ricky was doing better and was even beginning to take short walks now.

Alice glanced at her watch and started packing for New York. She had to catch a plane in a little over an hour. She tried to call when she got to the airport and once again when her plane landed in New York, but Ricky was asleep both times. Alice finally got to talk to her the next morning.

"Hello," came that early-morning croak.

Alice held the phone for a moment while tears formed in the corners of her eyes. The sound of that sleepy, husky voice almost took her breath away. Alice cleared her throat and cursed her father one more time for sending her on this hopeless search for fashion merchandising expertise.

"Good morning," Alice said finally, so brimming with emotion that she could barely speak. "How do you feel?"

"I'm okay. Jesus, it's good to hear your voice."

There was no way Alice could hold the tears back now; they flowed freely before she could reach for a Kleenex to stop them. "God, Ricky," she whispered with a sniff. "I thought I'd lost you." She eased down on the edge of the bed. "You sound so good. I can hardly believe it."

"Every bone in my body still hurts, and Sharon's driving me positively crazy. Other than that, I'm fine."

"Just put up with her for a few more days." Alice dabbed her eyes again in an attempt to save her mascara. *I've got her back,* she thought as the familiar fluttering in her stomach returned.

"I . . . I've lost my band," Ricky said after a moment. "Stan . . ." Whatever else she was going to say never materialized.

"I'm so sorry, baby." Alice sniffed again. "I know you miss him. I miss him too."

"It's more than that . . . it's . . ."

"Just try to get well," Alice said. "That's the important thing right now. When you're able to travel I'm coming to get you."

"I can't let you do that," Ricky whispered. "You're not ready for me like this. *I'm* not ready for me like this."

Alice felt her body tense as a tingling sensation raced through her. "What does that mean?"

"I woke up to nothing, Alice. No band. No future. No Stan. Nothing."

"You have me."

"And what do you have?"

"I have you. We have each other."

"You've got a lover who sleeps all day and can barely tie her shoes at the moment."

"I'll tie them for you. Don't do this, Ricky."

"My band's gone, Alice. Don't you realize what that means? There's this big chunk of me that's missing now. I'm no good to either of us this way. Not yet. I need to get my shit together first."

"You'll get your shit together with me," Alice said. "That's what lovers do. That's what it's all about. I'll help you." There was a pause, and Alice could hear Ricky breathing on the other end.

"I don't want you to see me this way," Ricky whispered. "Floundering around. Waking up in the morning with no place to go. No rehearsals or gigs or job. No nothing." Her voice trailed off into that hoarse hollow sound that Alice knew so well. "I was a somebody when we found each other, and I have to get that back."

Alice heard the determination in Ricky's voice, and didn't like it at all. "You're a somebody *now*, for crissake!"

"You're not listening to me," Ricky said with a sigh.

"Because you're not making any sense." Alice stuffed the Kleenex in her skirt pocket. "Do you think you're the only one hurting here? I'm hurting too. The accident affected a lot of people, Ricky. We all lost something because of it." She rubbed the bridge of her nose and could almost feel the tension pressing against her fingertips. "As soon as you're well enough, you're coming to New Orleans. That's settled right now, okay? I want to take care of you. I *need* to take care of you. For once in your life let someone do something for you."

"This is different, Al. If I went to New Orleans with you, I'd be everything Christine thinks I already am. I'll never let that happen."

"So what are you saying? And what the hell does Christine have to do with this?"

"I'm not ready to go to New Orleans yet. I just need some time."

Alice closed her eyes and massaged her temples. She knew she could talk her into anything once they were together again. A little rest and some creative pampering would do Ricky a world of good. *All I want is to be able to hold her,* Alice thought. *Everything else will take care of itself.*

PART THREE

Ricky

Chapter Thirteen

During her first week away at the beach, Ricky did nothing but sleep. Her headaches weren't so bad, but she was constantly aware of a worn, abused body that hadn't fully recovered from the accident. Once she finally dragged herself out of bed and began going for walks again, she started feeling better.

She couldn't remember anything about the accident, but the shock of losing her band was with her every waking moment. Even more unsettling than a few bruises and the dull ache in her head were the tears that came without warning. She almost preferred those marathon naps. At least in her sleep she didn't cry.

She had rented a weather-beaten cottage right away and forced herself to get dressed every morning. The accommodations were sparse but adequate: bedroom, kitchenette, bathroom, and color TV. She'd emptied one of her savings accounts before leaving San Antonio, so money wouldn't be a problem for a while. She knew people would be looking for her once they realized she was gone — her father, Alice, Joe, and probably even Dora — but she wasn't ready to see anyone yet, and she wasn't quite sure how long it would take before any of that changed.

Everything was still so confusing. Ricky never knew what day it was any longer, and she missed Alice more than she ever thought possible. So many things had been left unfinished, as if she'd started a good book only to lose it after a few chapters. Nothing seemed to make sense, and she was convinced that with the music gone, so was that vital part of her life, that spark that had always made everything good between her and Alice. The band was what had made their connection work. Ricky couldn't imagine life without Alice or life without her band. They were inseparable somehow, each unable to stand alone on their own merits.

Ricky sat down on the warm concrete bench and looked out at the water. The Gulf breeze was strong and whipped the hair out of her eyes. Stan was dead and she'd been robbed of the chance to say good-bye to him. The emptiness was overwhelming. Hot Check would never play another song together. There'd been no farewell performance. No last verse. No final chord. Ricky leaned back and rested her head on the top of the bench. She was tired of crying and too numb to think about it any more.

A few days later Ricky came back from a long walk on the beach. It was Saturday, the beginning of her second week there, and she was still tired all the time. The soreness was gone and her bruises had faded, but her clothes were loose on her small frame.

The weekends were the hardest. Not a minute went by that she didn't think of Alice or the band. None of that was getting any easier yet.

She took a shower and ran a brush through her hair. She gathered up all the spare change she could find and stuffed it in her pocket.

The hum of a clothes dryer made her feel less lonely as she separated coins into stacks and lined them up along the window near the pay phone. Joe answered on the fifth ring, and Ricky was so nervous that her knuckles were white from gripping the receiver so hard.

"Hi," she said. She leaned against the phone attached to the dirty wall; she hadn't realized until then that she was crying again.

"Ricky?" he said. "Where the hell *are* you?"

"It's Saturday, Joe." She couldn't say anything else. She didn't need to say anything else. Joe would know what Saturdays had meant for them: packed clubs and a natural high from shared energy. Saturdays had always been special.

"Hey, it's okay," he said gently. "It's okay. Where are you?"

She brushed the tears away with the back of her

hand. "Getting my shit together isn't as easy as I thought it would be."

"Where are you?" he asked again. "Just tell me. I'll be there in a heartbeat."

"I'm real tired, Joe. The days are all running together."

"You have to call Alice. She's frantic, Ricky. She's a goddamn basket case."

"I can't," she said. Just hearing Alice's name started an aching in her chest. "I've gotta go."

"No! Don't hang up! What's your number? Where are you?"

"I can't talk right now. I'll call you later." She hung up and gathered the rest of her change and stuffed it in her pocket. She dried her eyes on her shirtsleeve and went back to the beach.

Joe tore his house up looking for Alice's telephone number in New Orleans. He called her as soon as he found it, but there was no answer at her apartment. He didn't think she'd be at the office on a Saturday morning, but he gave it a try anyway. Her secretary said she was there, but in a meeting.

"Tell her it's Joe and it's very important."

Alice was on the line several seconds later. "What's wrong? Have you found her?"

"She called me a few minutes ago."

Alice felt certain her heart had stopped beating. She leaned against Gloria's desk and turned away from her. "Where is she, Joe?" she asked in a strained, unusually calm voice. "Where the hell is she?"

"I don't know. She wouldn't tell me."

"What did she say?"

"She's tired and she sounded really down. She fell apart when I mentioned you. Shit. You know how she gets when she cries."

Alice was so relieved just hearing that Ricky was all right, that it almost didn't matter that she'd called someone else instead of her.

"I guess she still needs more time," he offered lamely.

"More time for what? Tell me that! More time for what?"

"How the fuck do I know? She said she'd call me again later."

When Alice hung up she turned to Gloria, who was discreetly minding her own business at the computer. "Please get Dora Martinez on the phone for me," she said. Her father was waiting in her office, but he'd just have to wait.

Alice moved to the window and opened the blinds so she could see outside. Tourists with bags in hand cluttered the sidewalk and streets. Her thoughts drifted back to the day a few weeks ago when she had returned from the seminar in New York.

She'd flown to Dallas, at her father's request, to brief him on everything she had learned in New York. Alice had been ecstatic about being able to soon see Ricky again, and the meeting her father had insisted on only served to make her impatient and angry. Alice had cut him off as short as she dared and caught the next flight out.

The moment she arrived home, she knew something was wrong. Sharon was alone at the condo and very upset.

"How's Ricky?" Alice had asked. "What's the matter?"

Sharon just stood near the sofa wringing her hands. "She's not here. We don't know where she is."

"Has she been going for longer walks? Is she doing better?"

"I went out grocery shopping yesterday," Sharon said, "and when I came back she was gone. Henry and Joe have been looking for her. They were out all last night and all day today."

Alice searched the place in a whirlwind of fury. She went to the music room and noticed that the keyboard Ricky usually worked at was missing. She tore open drawers and closets in their bedroom; some of Ricky's clothes were gone as well. Alice snatched up the note that had been left for her on the neatly made bed. It was brief, written in a hurry, and made absolutely no sense to her whatsoever.

I need some time, Al. I love you. Ricky

Alice was still clutching the note when Henry arrived a few minutes later. The mere sight of him infuriated her.

"Where's my lover?" she asked through clenched teeth.

"I don't know," he said. His graying hair was scrambled, and his tanned, handsome face had a healthy stubble. "I talked to the police, and they won't do anything for twenty-four hours. No signs of foul play. She left on her own," he said as he collapsed on the sofa. "Joe and I've been up all night looking for her."

"Some of her equipment's gone," Alice seethed. "How could she move all of that stuff by herself without anyone seeing her, for crissake! You promised to take care of her, you son of a bitch!"

"Don't blame this on *me*," he said, his blue eyes narrowing against her anger. "Ricky's got a mind of her own and does pretty much what she wants to!"

"She was unconscious for three days, Henry. She has no business being anywhere but here."

"Don't you think I know that?" he said, his voice rising above hers. "She was depressed. We did the best we could, so don't stand there accusing *me* of anything! Where were *you* all this time?" he countered. "Gallivanting around New York doing God knows what with God knows whom. Don't blame me because you weren't here when she needed you!"

Alice turned when she heard Gloria calling her. She went over to the desk and picked up the phone.

"Dora," she said more calmly than she felt. "She called Joe a few minutes ago, but she wouldn't tell him where she was."

"Her father thinks she's somewhere in the Corpus area," Dora said. "That's where I'm focusing right now, but she's not making this easy."

"I don't know how much longer I can go on," Alice whispered. "Find her, Dora. You have to find her."

Chapter Fourteen

Ricky's headaches were less frequent, but her dreams had become exhausting. The last three times she'd fallen asleep she'd waked up in a cold sweat, gasping for air.

She crawled out of bed in a Fleetwood Mac T-shirt and a pair of cutoffs and found a small can of orange juice in the refrigerator. She glanced over at the keyboard on the table but still couldn't quite get up the courage to touch it. She closed her eyes and pushed damp hair away from her forehead.

"What do you plan on doing for the rest of your

life?" she whispered as she slumped against the cool refrigerator.

Ricky woke up around nine the next morning and lay in bed staring at the yellowed ceiling for several minutes before getting dressed and gathering more change. She went down to the laundry room and called Joe again.

"Hi. It's me."

"Ricky," he said with relief. "Where are you? And don't hang up!"

"I'm sorry about the other day."

"You sound better. I've got a surprise for you," he said. "I've been trying to get another band together. I've got some good musicians lined up. I think you should hear 'em."

Her vision blurred as hot tears rolled down her cheeks. *Where do they come from so quickly?*

"Ricky? Did you hear me?"

"Yeah," she said, her voice rough with emotion. "I'm not ready for this yet."

"Like hell you're not."

Spinning washers and tumbling dryers forced her to speak up. "I feel like maybe that part of my life's over. Like it's gone forever, you know?"

"Gone? Are you nuts? I'm getting calls all day long! People are lined up outside your condo waiting for you to come home. You can't buy a fucking Hot Check recording anywhere in the country! You *can't* quit. They wouldn't let you even if you wanted to."

"Jesus," she said with a sniff and dabbed her eyes on the sleeve of her shirt.

"Once I get a good band behind you again, you'll

be fine," he said. "Let me worry about that, okay? Now tell me where you are. I can load up the girls and get them there for your approval any time. Just say the word."

"What girls?" The operator came on the line and requested more money. Ricky dropped a stack of change in the slot. "What girls?" she asked again.

"I found a bass player and a keyboard player that I know you'll like," he said with excitement. "They've been around a long time. Both fresh from San Francisco. I've got some calls out for a lead guitar too. We should all get together and see what happens."

"A keyboard player?" Ricky said. "What the hell do I need with a keyboard player?"

"I've got some ideas I'd like to go over with you. Tell me where you are so we can talk." Ricky heard something strange in his voice; it broke once and he cleared his throat. "Please," he whispered. "Tell me where you are. I miss you."

"I miss you too." Ricky leaned against the wall and clutched the receiver tightly. The washer and dryer had stopped, and the silence in the laundry room only added to her somber mood. "Jesus, Joe. What are we gonna do?"

"We'll rebuild this band," he said. "Maybe launch you solo. The offers I've gotten so far are leaning in that direction. Either way we decide to go, I'll manage you and we'll make piles of money." He laughed suddenly. "Now tell me where the fuck you are, you little shit!"

Ricky knew that if she told him, he'd be there in less than three hours, and she wasn't ready to deal with that yet.

"Have you at least called Alice?" he asked. "You'll feel better once you get that straightened out."

"I'm not sure I'll ever feel better again. Look, I've gotta go. I'll call you again soon." Even as she was hanging up, Ricky could hear him cussing at her and begging her to tell him where she was. She stayed in the laundry room for a while, propped against the wall. *He's getting a new band together for me . . . strangers playing my music. How can he even think of such a thing?*

Joe was on the phone with Alice as soon as Ricky hung up. "She sounded better this time," he said, "but she still wouldn't tell me where she was. I thought I heard seagulls in the background though. Maybe that'll help."

"Thank you," Alice said. "Why, Joe? Why is she doing this?" *Why is she calling you and not me?* she wanted to scream.

"We talked about you a little," he said. "She gets upset very easily. She doesn't know why the fuck she's doing it either."

Alice called Dora and relayed the information Joe had given her. She felt as though nothing would ever be right in her life again. Maybe Ricky would never come back.

"Dora, you have to find her. I don't know how much more of this I can take."

"I'm pretty sure she's around Rockport somewhere," Dora said. "Her father gave me a few leads this morning. He's heading down there tomorrow to look for her. Hopefully I'll have something for you in a day or two. Please, Alice. Just take it easy."

"Easy? I'm scared, goddamn it!"

"Of course you're scared. She's probably scared too. My hunch is she's trying to get her head together before she does anything else."

"Great. Just great."

"I'm leaving for the coast again this afternoon. I'll call you as soon as I know something."

Ricky considered Joe's suggestion about getting a new band together, but the thought of being on stage with strangers seemed impossible. She couldn't imagine herself doing such a thing. And Joe had mentioned something about finding someone for keyboard. What the hell did she need with a keyboard player? Ricky called him again the next day, and he sounded even more frustrated than before.

"I've gotta tell these people something, damn it!" he yelled into the phone. "I can't manage you if I can't fucking *find* you!"

"Other people will be playing our music, Joe. How can you be so ho-hum about this?"

"How? Because I have to, that's how." He lowered his voice. "Look, Ricky. Stan's gone and Kyle's nowhere to be found, but I'm here. Hot Check's something I've gotta be a part of whether or not I ever play another note for you. Can't you understand how important that is? Don't take this away from me. Let's just give it a chance, okay? Don't fight me so hard. I'm on your side."

The tears were back, silently reminding her of

how little control she had over anything. "I hate this, Joe."

"I know you do."

"How's your hand?" she asked with a sniff.

"It's there. That's about all I can say."

"Still no feeling?" Ricky heard him sigh before he answered.

"Some of us are moving on with our lives, Ricky. I sold my guitars so I could pay my fucking bills. Now when are you coming back? We've got work to do. Musicians to find. Money to make. Places to see and people to do."

"Maybe if we could get Kyle back," she said. *Something familiar...being on stage again with someone I know.*

"Kyle? Where in the fuck am I supposed to find Kyle?"

"I don't know," Ricky said. "The same place you're looking for guitar players. It shouldn't be too hard to find him."

"He disappeared quicker than you did. I've got another drummer lined up already," Joe said, dismissing the idea immediately. "Kyle's done pissed me off."

"So?" Ricky said. "I want him. I won't even consider doing anything without him."

"Listen to me, Ricky."

"No. You listen to *me*. I need Kyle. No Kyle, no band. I've got a friend in San Antonio who can help you find him," she said. "Her name's Dora Martinez."

Joe groaned in frustration before yelling, "Dora Martinez? You're kidding me, right? This is just out-goddamn-standing, Ricky! Jesus fucking Christ.

You want *her* to find Kyle? Hell, Dora Martinez can't even find *you!*"

Monday evening Alice was in her office, knee-deep in reviewing the end-of-month reports, when Gloria informed her that Christine Marlow was waiting to see her. Alice sighed. She had avoided Christine's telephone calls as best she could over the past few weeks, at times being annoyingly unsuccessful, but there wasn't much she could do if she showed up at the office.

"Send her in," Alice said. She stood up and straightened a few papers on her desk. The door opened, and a confident but moody Christine sauntered in.

"You've been avoiding me, Alice," she said. Her fingers and throat glittered with jewelry, adding immeasurably to her tangerine-colored skirt and blouse.

Alice shrugged, choosing not to deny anything. "As you can see, I've been busy. Have a seat."

"I haven't seen you in so long," Christine said, "and since it's impossible to get you on the phone, I thought I might just fly to New Orleans for the day and give it a more personal touch."

"You've caught me at a really bad time."

"When isn't it a bad time these days?" Christine shifted in her chair and cocked her head attentively. "Things haven't been the same since that awful day we had lunch."

Alice put her hands up to stop any further

mention of the subject. "Friends, Christine. That's it. You either accept that, or forget the whole thing."

"That's why I'm here. I want whatever you're willing to give me."

That sounds pathetic, Alice thought.

"You look tired, Alice. Are you okay?"

"It's Ricky. And work. Mostly Ricky."

"Still no word from her?"

"Nothing. I have Dora working on it."

"She's a fool."

"Dora?" Alice asked, attempting a smile.

"No, not Dora!" They stared at each other for a few moments before Christine looked away. "Do you have room for me, or should I get a hotel for the night?"

"I have room for you," Alice said, "but I think it would be better if you stayed somewhere else."

"Don't trust yourself to be alone with me?" Christine asked with a chuckle.

"That's the least of my worries. I have a lot of work to do. I'm afraid you'll have to entertain yourself while you're here."

"Not even dinner tonight? I promise to behave. Please, Alice. We've been friends a long time. Let's not throw it all away."

"My parents are coming in tomorrow, and I have a lot of work to do before they get here. You really should've called first." Alice felt a twinge of guilt once the words were out, knowing full well that if Christine had called, she would've found an excuse not to talk to her. "It'll be late when I'm finished here. I'm sorry."

"Late's fine," Christine said. "Please, Alice. You'll see that I only want us to be friends. We can have a quiet dinner somewhere. I have oodles of things to tell you."

"This is —"

"And by the way," Christine continued, "there aren't any good rooms available in town. The Saints are doing football things this weekend."

"Then it sounds like you have a problem, doesn't it?"

"Alice, please. I don't want it to be this way. We're friends. I've already promised to be on my best behavior."

Alice wasn't sure she could get her to leave without giving in. She glanced at the stack of work on her desk. "This is really a bad time for me." She scribbled down the address to her condo and found an extra set of keys in her purse. "I'm not sure when I'll be there. Like I said, I have a lot of work to do and you'll have to entertain yourself."

Christine caught the keys Alice tossed her. "I'll see you later."

Chapter Fifteen

Ricky came back from a walk just before dark and found Dora waiting for her. In a way it was such a relief to finally have her there. Now she could stop looking for her everywhere.

"Hi," Ricky said, giving her a long hug. "How's Marge and the kids?" She smiled tiredly and hugged her again.

"Everybody's fine," Dora said. "The last time I saw you we weren't sure if you'd make it or not. You feeling okay?"

"Yes. I'm fine." Ricky unlocked the door and held

it open for her. "The headaches finally stopped." She motioned toward the only chair in the tiny room.

"Are you planning on coming back any time soon?"

"I don't know," Ricky said. She sat down on the end of the bed.

"How patient do you expect Alice to be?" Dora asked.

Ricky's stomach did a little flip at the mention of Alice's name.

"You're holding all the cards, kid. Don't you think Alice deserves better than this?"

Ricky felt warm all over, as if a previously unknown source of energy had suddenly been released from somewhere.

"Are you involved with someone else?" Dora asked, glancing around the room.

"You know better than that."

Dora shrugged and took a small notebook out of her jacket pocket. "I've always liked you, Ricky, but you're hurting someone who means a lot to me. Why the hell are you here?"

Ricky shrugged. "There's this part of me that isn't ready to deal with Alice yet," she said. She tugged at a thread on the dingy bedspread. "My career's a pile of shit right now. I have to fix that before I see her again."

"Alice has nothing to do with your work."

Ricky tousled her hair and then leaned back on her elbows. "But my work has everything to do with how Alice relates to me." She looked away as a tear rolled down her cheek. "When Alice and I first got together I knew what she saw in me. My music and the band were all tied up in this sexual thing. She never expected to be happy with me, Dora. That surprised her." Ricky leaned her head back and shook the hair out of her eyes. "The little pizzazz the band had isn't there any more. I've never been without it before, and it's a very scary thing for me."

Dora stretched out her legs and crossed them at the ankles. "You don't think you're good enough for her unless you have a band. Is that it?"

Ricky didn't say anything. Her chest felt heavy all of a sudden.

"What a bunch of crapola," Dora said. "If you truly believe that, then maybe you *aren't* good enough for her!"

Ricky stared at her. "That's a chicken-shit thing to say, Dora. I don't intend to stay this emotional degenerate forever, but right now I haven't got a clue what's going on with me. My head's all fucked up."

"Alice wants to help you. She deserves that chance." Dora flipped through a few pages in the notebook. "My job was to find you. I'll have to tell Alice where you are, of course." She looked up at her with a crinkled brow and then sat up in her chair. "Is this what the accident did to you? It sounds like someone's been using your self-esteem for a punching bag, Ricky, and that really doesn't make any sense to me. You've got a lover who's crazy about you. You're a recognized recording artist, a respected writer —"

"Don't forget my nice hair and big tits," Ricky said dryly.

Dora nodded and chuckled. "That goes without saying."

Ricky pulled at the thread on the bedspread again. "I know all that, Dora. I've been whining and sniveling ever since the accident. I'm here feeling sorry for myself so no one else has to put up with it."

"You're alive, Ricky. Don't you realize how lucky you are?" The silence was sobering as they looked at each other. "Stan didn't get this chance. Over these last few weeks I've wanted nothing more than to find you just so I could shake the living shit out of you for leaving that way," Dora said slowly. "You've hit a rough stretch in the road right now, and —"

"Losing Stan is more than a fucking bump in the road for me," Ricky whispered. "I lost one of my best friends, Dora. Not to mention my band . . . the way I make my living . . . one of the only reasons I get up every morning. It's all gone."

"And here you are shutting out everyone who wants to help you. Maturity isn't one of your strong points, I take it."

"I guess not," Ricky said, beginning to get angry.

"I see," Dora said. "With your talent gone and no resources available to you any longer, I guess it's a good thing you've got those big tits and all that nice hair to fall back on." Dora's tone was softer, and Ricky could see the concern in her dark eyes. "You came here to think and get it all sorted out, but that hasn't happened yet. You're thinking about the wrong things right now, Ricky. Running away hasn't worked, has it?"

"Tell me what to do, Dora."

"You've had us all very worried."

"I know," Ricky whispered. "So tell me what to do."

"Alice needs to see you."

Just the thought of seeing Alice again terrified her. "How is she?" Ricky asked.

"How would you be if Alice had been missing for three weeks?" Dora glanced around the cottage. "Where's your phone? We'll give her a call."

"I don't have a phone."

"No phone?" Dora said incredulously. "What kind of place is this?"

"There's a pay phone in the laundry room across the driveway. How is she, Dora? How much damage have I done?"

"You're the only one who can assess that. She's more hurt than pissed, though. And that's never good. Come on. Let's go." On her way out of the cottage Dora said, "Just so you'll know a little about what's going on, in addition to your falling off the face of the earth, she's had to put up with shit from your father. He called her a fucking dyke one night, and they've had several fights about whose fault it was that you're gone. He blamed her and she blamed him. They started speaking again only a few days ago."

"My father called her a *what*?" Ricky said with eyes wide. "You're not kidding, are you? Holy shit."

"Holy shit's right. He can be very unscrupulous where you're concerned."

They crossed the driveway to crunching oyster shell under sneakered feet and entered the laundry room to a symphony of rinse cycles and tumbling dryers. Dora dialed Alice's home number and had the charges billed to her own telephone number in San Antonio. Once the phone started ringing, she handed the receiver over to Ricky.

"You're on, kid." Dora walked to the end of a row of washers to give her some privacy. Ricky held the receiver in a shaking hand.

161

"Hello," a woman's voice said.

"Hello. Who is this?" There was a brief pause.

"Ricky!" Christine said. "Imagine hearing from you like this!"

"What are you doing there?" Ricky managed to ask. A shade of doom lowered itself over her entire being. "Where's Alice? Is she there?"

"She's in the shower, love. I was just on my way to see if she needed anything."

"What's the matter?" Ricky heard Dora asking, but she waved her away. Ricky felt sure she would be sick at any second.

"How long have you been there?" Ricky whispered.

"That's none of your business."

"Who are you talking to?" Dora demanded.

"You're lying," Ricky growled into the telephone. "You bitch. I know you're lying."

"Not at all," Christine said. "We might even get around to the intimate little dinner I've thrown together."

Ricky hung up on her and grabbed Dora's wrist to look at her watch. It was nine o'clock.

"Who was it?" Dora barked.

"Christine. When was the last time you talked to Alice?"

"Yesterday. And I saw Christine the day before in San Antonio. Take it easy. We'll find out what's going on." Dora dug around in her jacket pocket and retrieved her small notebook. She deposited another quarter and again had the charges billed to her home number. After twenty rings she hung up.

"No answer at her office," Dora said. She got her quarter back and went through the same process to

162

get Alice's home number again. "The line's busy at her apartment."

"She's lying," Ricky grumbled. "The bitch is lying."

"What did Christine say?"

"It doesn't matter. Jesus, I don't believe this." Once back in the cottage Ricky began throwing clothes in a suitcase. "Can you take me to the airport in Corpus?"

"Sure. You're going to New Orleans, I hope."

"Of course I'm going to New Orleans! Where else would I go?"

"I don't know," Dora said. "I'm not sure. Flights to New Orleans at this time of night are probably pretty scarce around here. You'd get there faster if you just drove."

Ricky threw open the tiny closet door to find something else to wear. She yanked clothes off hangers and held them up to her.

"Come on, Ricky. You're getting upset over nothing," Dora said gently. "Alice is spending a fortune looking for you."

"Get real, Dora. That was yesterday."

Alice got home a little after nine-thirty that evening. She'd finished going over the reports she was certain her father would quiz her about. Things were looking good at the office.

She smelled something cooking as soon as she opened the door, but she was feeling much too tired to be sociable. The lights were dim, and soft music drifted from the stereo. Alice turned on all remaining lights within reach and proceeded to make herself a drink. Christine came out of the kitchen dressed in some sort of pale yellow nightgown.

"Smells good," Alice said. "Find something to do today?"

"No need to worry about me," Christine said. "Dinner should be ready in about ten minutes."

Alice noticed that the dining room table was set for two, complete with candles and wine glasses. She slipped her shoes off and took her drink to the sofa where she began to relax for the first time all day. Alice would've preferred to just go to bed, with full knowledge that she needed to be fresh in the morning when her parents arrived. She viewed Christine as an intrusion to her usual routine, and Alice had no urge to entertain at the moment.

"What are we having?" she asked.

"Lasagna, a masterpiece of a salad, and potent garlic bread." Christine joined her on the opposite end of the sofa and rested her arm seductively along the back. "You look beat. Are these your usual hours?"

"Only when my father's in town. Dinner had better hurry. I'm fading fast."

Christine laughed and went to the kitchen, returning to the table with a bubbling dish and various other delicacies. Alice rose from the sofa to uncork the wine. Christine had dimmed the lights and lit the candles, but Alice switched more lights on during each trip Christine made to the kitchen.

"You said you had oodles to tell me."

Christine filled their wine glasses and smiled as Alice tended to their plates. "Remember the flight attendant I was seeing? She wants to move in with me."

"And how do you feel about that?"

"She's talking about quitting her job and going back to school. I think she's looking for a place to roost."

During dinner they talked about New Orleans and Alice's job. Christine caught her up on the latest gossip about mutual friends and filled their glasses with the last of the wine. She proposed a toast to friendship, which made Alice feel a little better. It was almost a relief to laugh again; to be able to just sit down and talk to someone and carry on a normal conversation.

"I'd forgotten what an excellent cook you are," Alice said.

"Oh, but I'm afraid I've totally destroyed your kitchen in the process."

"Ricky likes to cook too."

The silence hung in the air between them like a deadly lingering cloud. They'd talked about everything and everyone except Ricky. Christine folded her napkin and placed it on the table.

"How long will you wait for her?"

"As long as I'm in love with her," Alice replied.

"She's left you, Alice."

"I don't believe that."

Christine began stacking their plates and collecting the empty wine glasses. "Let's do the dishes."

"Leave them," Alice said. She was too tired to be domestic right now.

"Come on. I'll wash and you dry."

Christine slid the dishes into the hot soapy water and scrubbed the cold remnants of mozzarella cheese away. "This has been good for me, Alice. Thank you for letting me stay."

"It's been good for me too. I've missed having someone to talk to. I don't have any friends here." She held the clean, dripping plate by its edges and dried it carefully with the small towel. "Even if I had friends I wouldn't have time to spend with them anyway, so I guess it doesn't really matter."

"Get out more," Christine said. "You can't work at this pace forever. Make time for yourself."

"You sound like Dora."

"Sometimes Dora makes sense." Christine rinsed the remaining wine glass and wiped the counter with a sponge. She inspected her long, polished nails and tucked an imaginary stray curl into her impeccable hairdo. "Are you coming back to San Antonio any time soon?"

"Maybe. Another month and I'll be able to get out more."

Christine dropped the sponge in the sink and then turned around. "You really are in love with her, aren't you?"

Alice opened the cabinet to set the wine glasses in their usual place. "Why does that still surprise you?" She switched off the light in the kitchen and blew the candles out on the dining room table. Alice stood up straight and looked at her steadily. "Having your blessing on my choice of lovers isn't a priority of mine."

"Alice, I —"

"We should have plenty of time for breakfast on the way to the airport if we're up by six," Alice said. "I'll see you in the morning."

Chapter Sixteen

Alice returned Christine's hug before letting her board the plane. Conversation at breakfast had been full of generic nonsense. Alice even promised to return an occasional phone call.

She had several more cups of coffee and met her parents' plane an hour and a half later. At some point before they left the next day, Alice planned to tell them she was a lesbian. The time was right, and she was tired of playing games.

"We were fogged in at Houston," Mrs. Collins explained as she kissed Alice on the cheek. She wore a gray dress with a string of pearls. Her white hair gave her a distinguished look that Alice found endearing. She often wondered if her own hair would some day be that color.

"I had to drop a friend off anyway," Alice said. "Do you two need to freshen up, or are we off and running?"

"We're ready," her father said.

She took them on the grand tour of her stores. At first Alice tried showing them only the things that appeared to be finished, but as the day wore on and her father's questions became more specific, projects that weren't quite ready had to be revealed. From there Alice went into intricate detail about some of her ideas and hopes for the future, along with a step-by-step breakdown of how she planned to go about accomplishing things. Once he stopped asking questions she started to worry. He was either very pleased or else was forming ideas of his own to put a stop to what she was doing. Alice would just have to wait and see which way he was going with it.

"You look thinner, dear," her mother commented over dinner that evening. The restaurant was crowded and noisy but expensive enough to keep the tourists away. "Haven't you been feeling well?"

"I've been busy." Alice smiled and accepted the champagne her father offered to her. She was exhausted. "There's still so much to do. I fired the group we had working on the inventory. They were robbing us blind."

Mr. Collins chuckled. "I'm very pleased with the

169

young man who replaced you in San Antonio. He's doing a fine job."

"I'm glad it worked out," Alice said as she sipped her champagne and dunked a boiled shrimp into a red sauce.

"We're looking forward to having you back in Dallas with us again," Mrs. Collins said. "We've both missed you. It takes an act of Congress just to get you to come and visit."

"Why would I be going back to Dallas?" *This is news.* Her ears perked up.

"I'm thinking about retiring in January," Alice heard her father saying. "I'm not getting any younger. The company needs some fresh blood. Besides, I'm tired and ready for a change."

"You said a year," Alice reminded him calmly, much more calmly than she felt.

"You've more than proven yourself," he said with a wave of his hand. "Everything I've asked has been accomplished above and beyond my expectations." He laughed again and drained his glass. "I'll give you until the end of December to implement your ideas and get this place in shape before you hand it over to someone else."

Alice was speechless and set her drink down before she dropped it. Was it really supposed to be this easy?

"This is kind of sudden. You said a year. You promised me a year." She met her father's gaze and didn't like the way he was smiling at her. She was confused. *What's going on here? Is this another test? A game? One more way to see how I handle the pressure?*

"Alice," her mother chided. "You're taking this much too seriously. Just because your father says he'll retire doesn't mean he'll be able to stay away for any length of time. I'll believe it when I see it."

Alice took a gulp of champagne and looked over at him again. "Then should I just more or less consider your retirement as a series of three-day weekends? Or will I actually be the head honcho?" She set her glass down and decided not to drink any more. That last gulp had done the trick. She knew the look in his eyes. He enjoyed getting her riled up. They hadn't played this game in years. "Whatever you decide will be fine with me," she said in a crisp and decisive tone. She refused to be intimidated. He could retire tomorrow and she'd do his goddamn job better than he ever thought possible. "But I'll have to move corporate headquarters to San Antonio."

"Corporate headquarters has to stay in Dallas," he said.

They continued this conversation all through dinner and were still going at it over a drink at Alice's apartment. She poured herself a Diet Coke but decided to carry it rather than drink it. She'd gotten her father to admit that if she moved the main office to San Antonio, then he wouldn't be able to keep tabs on things the way he'd hoped to after his retirement.

"Let's not use the word *retire* so loosely here, Dad. It's not what you have in mind at all, is it? If you want to travel, then travel. You already said the company runs itself." She leaned forward with an exaggerated shrug and smiled. "So let it run itself while you're in Europe. I can take care of whatever comes up." Smirking ever so slightly, she added, "But don't dangle a job in front of me that you never intend for me to have."

Her mother lowered her eyes and tugged on the string of pearls at her throat. Alice took both of her parents in at a glance and knew she'd hit home.

"I'll finish up what I've started here, but I won't go to Dallas. It's always been convenient having everything right there, but it's not really necessary." She waited a moment for his objections, but he didn't seem to have any. "I also plan on asking for my old job back once things are running smoothly here. I have more experience in restaurant management, and I'm more comfortable with that. Besides, you're no more ready to retire than I am."

"Not true, young lady," he said wearily. "I haven't had a vacation in fifteen years. I'm tired."

"So go on vacation," Alice said. "Take a few months off. You'll feel like a new person when you get back."

The doorbell rang as she was fixing him another drink. Alice glanced at the grandfather clock across the room and noticed that it was only a few minutes after eight. She opened the door and felt her heart leap into her throat. Ricky stood there in a gray cotton shirt that was casually unbuttoned at the top and neatly tucked into new black jeans. She looked positively stunning.

"Hi," Ricky said. After a moment she asked, "Can I come in?"

Alice managed to open the door farther and move out of the way.

"Ricky!" Mrs. Collins said delightedly. "How are you?"

"I'm fine. It's good to see you again."

"You're thinner too," Mrs. Collins said as she held Ricky at arm's length to get a better look at her. "You girls aren't taking care of yourselves."

Ricky turned around to see Alice still holding the door open. It was quiet. Much too quiet. Ricky suddenly felt about as welcome as measles in an orphanage. The tension in the air was unbelievable.

"Can you excuse us for a minute?" Alice said before taking Ricky by the hand and dragging her into the kitchen.

They were in each other's arms quickly, both visibly shaking.

"Thank God you're all right," Alice said in a tremulous whisper. "Where the hell have you been?" She held Ricky's face in her hands. "I can't believe you're really here."

"I can't believe your *parents* are here," Ricky said.

Alice grabbed her in another anxious, bone-crushing hug and kissed the top of Ricky's head over and over again.

"Christ," she muttered. "You're right. My parents are here." Alice hugged her again. "God, I've missed you." The weeks began melting away as she touched Ricky's hair and rubbed her cheek against it frantically. Tears were threatening.

"As much as I'd like to, we can't stay in here very long," Ricky said. She straightened the collar on Alice's blouse and watched as her eyes filled with tears.

"You didn't even know me the last time I saw you," Alice said. A sob caught in her throat, and Ricky put her arms around her again.

"You can't do that now, Alice," Ricky whispered.

She stepped back away from her. "Please tell me they aren't staying here with you tonight."

"No," Alice said with a sniff. "They keep a condo on the sixth floor."

"Come on," Ricky said. She kissed her lightly on the lips. "I'm going out there and bullshit with them for a few minutes while you work on pulling yourself together."

She left the kitchen, and Alice could hear her mother's voice almost immediately.

"It's been a long time since we've seen you," Mrs. Collins said. "We were terribly sorry to hear about your friend and the accident. Are you feeling all right now?"

"I had a headache for several days, but I'm okay," Ricky said.

"What are you doing with yourself now?" Mr. Collins asked. "Do you still have your band?"

"I might be getting another one together soon. I'm not sure yet."

All three of them looked across the room as Alice came back in. Ricky could tell that she'd been crying, but hopefully her parents wouldn't notice.

Mr. Collins stretched and reached for his jacket draped across the back of the sofa. "We're meeting some friends downtown later. We should get going. Would you two like to join us?"

"No," Alice said, a bit more abruptly than was called for.

Mrs. Collins took Ricky's hand and squeezed it. "How long will be you in town, dear?"

"Probably quite a while."

"I hope everything works out for you," Mr.

Collins said. He nodded at his daughter. "Our plane leaves at nine in the morning."

"Yes, I know."

"You've done an excellent job here, Alice. We should start seeing a profit by the third quarter, wouldn't you say?"

"Maybe. Possibly later."

Mrs. Collins gave Alice a hug. "You're working too hard, dear. Get some rest. You look tired."

"I'm fine," Alice said. She opened the door for them as more good-byes were exchanged.

The moment the chattering stopped and the door closed, Ricky's pulse began to race. They were alone, and she suddenly felt nervous. Alice's stood very still, her hand resting on the knob, before turning around and leaning against the door.

"I have a question to ask you," Alice said, her tone crisp and glacial. "Now that I know you're not dead on the side of the road somewhere, I'm feeling very angry and am not sure what to do about it. But right now I need to know why you left."

"I told you why when you were in New York."

"You said nothing about leaving then," Alice said. "No phone call. No letter. No message. Nothing. Three weeks of nothing. Do you have any idea what you've put me through? Or Joe or your father? Any idea at all? At least Emily thought enough of *you* to send a postcard."

"That's a cheap shot, Alice. Didn't you get the note I left at the apartment?"

"The I-need-some-time-Al-I-love-you-Ricky note? And what did that explain?"

"I haven't enjoyed any of this either, Alice." Ricky

175

shook her head and tossed her shaggy hair out of her eyes. "I've spent three weeks looking for something I thought I'd lost, and I still don't know what the hell it is." She cleared her throat, the hoarseness in her voice giving away a flood of emotion. "I've got a question for you too." She looked up and then quickly brushed away a tear with the back of her hand. "What was Christine doing here last night?"

"How did you know Christine was here?"

"She answered the phone when I called."

"That's impossible. She would've told me."

Ricky stuck her hands in her pockets and took a deep breath. These acute pangs of jealousy were new to her, and she didn't like them at all. "She insinuated that you were sleeping with her." Their eyes met for a vivid, lingering moment before Ricky said, "I believed her for about two minutes, and I apologize for that. I know she's in love with you, and I let that cloud my judgment." Ricky went over to the end of the bar. "I'm tired, Alice. Nothing seems to work any more. I can't write. I'm crying and whining all the time. Everything's been all fucked up without you." She closed her eyes and felt very small and vulnerable all of a sudden, as though she were standing naked in a room full of mirrors. "I thought I could figure it all out and make it better on my own. If I fixed one thing at a time maybe there was hope for the rest of it."

"Come here, baby," Alice whispered. She reached for her and buried her face in Ricky's neck. They held each other for a moment, both trembling with emotion.

"Stan's dead," Ricky mumbled. "I woke up and he was dead, Alice. That part was *never* getting fixed and I didn't know what to do about it. I had to leave. Can't you see that? The sky was falling and I had to leave."

"Shh," Alice whispered as she held her. Kisses that started out slow and tender eventually grew into a deep, ardent merging of passion. Alice was overwhelmed by its intensity, but welcomed a rush of emotion that she'd never forget.

"And you," Ricky said as she covered Alice's face with a string of tiny kisses. "Dora made me see how selfish I've been by shutting you out. I never meant to do that."

"It's okay," Alice whispered. "It's okay. Let's go to bed so I can hold you."

Alice led the way and took Ricky in her arms as they curled up in the middle of the bed. They cried together and talked about Stan, Joe, Kyle, and the band. They eventually fell asleep and woke up later and made love. Alice held her afterward and knew in her heart that the worst was over.

The room was cold the next morning, and the cover from the bed was a scrambled mass of linen. Alice pulled Ricky on top of her and murmured into her hair, "We smell like sex."

"And a mighty fine smell that is." A series of slow, deep, passionate kisses followed. Ricky worked a leg in between Alice's, and they started the morning off properly.

"How could you think I'd ever sleep with Christine?" Alice asked. "Or anyone else for that matter?"

"She was very convincing on the phone," Ricky said. She touched the tip of her tongue to one of Alice's taut nipples. "And she was here and I was there. My imagination rapidly took over. Dora thought I was crazy."

"You were." Alice moved against her and ran her hands along Ricky's back, pulling her closer.

A while later after they both had recovered a bit, Alice said, "I have a present for you." She pointed toward the closet, and Ricky retrieved an oblong, festively wrapped box. She crawled under the covers and kissed Alice tenderly on the mouth.

"Open it," Alice whispered as she ran the tip of her finger over Ricky's bottom lip.

The bow came off, and lavender paper went flying everywhere. "Pink flamingos," Ricky said in her raggedy, early morning voice. Two pink plastic birds with metal spindle legs slid out of the box.

"They're for our new front yard when we find a house."

Ricky set the box and the birds aside and pulled Alice into her arms.

"Come with me to take my parents to the airport," Alice whispered as she nuzzled Ricky's bare throat and shoulder. They began moving against one another again.

"And have to explain to your mother why I'm wearing the same clothes? I don't think so."

Alice laughed. "She wouldn't say anything. Besides, I've decided to tell them about us before they leave today."

"What if your father fires you?" Ricky said. Her hands and lips moved down Alice's body under the covers. "Disowns you? Tries to ship you off to some foreign country for therapy?"

"He wouldn't dare," Alice said. "He needs me right now. He's going on vacation."

The flamingos hit the floor with a little clink, and Alice opened her legs to the insistent nudging of a chin between her thighs.

"We don't have time for this," Alice whispered weakly. She filled her hands with Ricky's soft blonde hair and urged her mouth and tongue forward. They had to get showers and find clothes. Make coffee and grab a quick breakfast. *We've got to take my parents to the goddamn airport, for crissake!*

"Jesus," she whispered as Ricky's mouth took her in and sucked her eagerly. So what if they were late? *Some things one just has to make time for.*

INNER CIRCLE by Claire McNab. 208 pp. 8th Carol Ashton
Mystery.   ISBN 1-56280-135-X   10.95

LESBIAN SEX: AN ORAL HISTORY by Susan Johnson.
240 pp. Need we say more?   ISBN 1-56280-142-2   14.95

BABY, IT'S COLD by Jaye Maiman. 256 pp. 5th Robin Miller
Mystery.   ISBN 1-56280-141-4   19.95

WILD THINGS by Karin Kallmaker. 240 pp. By the undisputed
mistress of lesbian romance.   ISBN 1-56280-139-2   10.95

THE GIRL NEXT DOOR by Mindy Kaplan. 208 pp. Just what
you'd expect.   ISBN 1-56280-140-6   11.95

NOW AND THEN by Penny Hayes. 240 pp. Romance on the
westward journey.   ISBN 1-56280-121-X   11.95

HEART ON FIRE by Diana Simmonds. 176 pp. The romantic and
erotic rival of *Curious Wine*.   ISBN 1-56280-152-X   11.95

DEATH AT LAVENDER BAY by Lauren Wright Douglas. 208 pp.
1st Allison O'Neil Mystery.   ISBN 1-56280-085-X   11.95

YES I SAID YES I WILL by Judith McDaniel. 272 pp. Hot
romance by famous author.   ISBN 1-56280-138-4   11.95

FORBIDDEN FIRES by Margaret C. Anderson. Edited by Mathilda
Hills. 176 pp. Famous author's "unpublished" Lesbian romance.
                                        ISBN 1-56280-123-6   21.95

SIDE TRACKS by Teresa Stores. 160 pp. Gender-bending
Lesbians on the road.   ISBN 1-56280-122-8   10.95

HOODED MURDER by Annette Van Dyke. 176 pp. 1st Jessie
Batelle Mystery.   ISBN 1-56280-134-1   10.95

WILDWOOD FLOWERS by Julia Watts. 208 pp. Hilarious and
heart-warming tale of true love.   ISBN 1-56280-127-9   10.95

NEVER SAY NEVER by Linda Hill. 224 pp. Rule #1: Never get involved
with . . .   ISBN 1-56280-126-0   10.95

THE SEARCH by Melanie McAllester. 240 pp. Exciting top cop
Tenny Mendoza case.   ISBN 1-56280-150-3   10.95

THE WISH LIST by Saxon Bennett. 192 pp. Romance through
the years.   ISBN 1-56280-125-2   10.95

FIRST IMPRESSIONS by Kate Calloway. 208 pp. P.I. Cassidy
James' first case.   ISBN 1-56280-133-3   10.95

OUT OF THE NIGHT by Kris Bruyer. 192 pp. Spine-tingling
thriller.   ISBN 1-56280-120-1   10.95

NORTHERN BLUE by Tracey Richardson. 224 pp. Police recruits
Miki & Miranda — passion in the line of fire. ISBN 1-56280-118-X   10.95

LOVE'S HARVEST by Peggy J. Herring. 176 pp. by the author of
Once More With Feeling.   ISBN 1-56280-117-1   10.95

THE COLOR OF WINTER by Lisa Shapiro. 208 pp. Romantic
love beyond your wildest dreams.   ISBN 1-56280-116-3   10.95

FAMILY SECRETS by Laura DeHart Young. 208 pp. Enthralling
romance and suspense.   ISBN 1-56280-119-8   10.95

INLAND PASSAGE by Jane Rule. 288 pp. Tales exploring conven-
tional & unconventional relationships.   ISBN 0-930044-56-8   10.95

DOUBLE BLUFF by Claire McNab. 208 pp. 7th Carol Ashton
Mystery.   ISBN 1-56280-096-5   10.95

BAR GIRLS by Lauran Hoffman. 176 pp. See the movie, read
the book!   ISBN 1-56280-115-5   10.95

THE FIRST TIME EVER edited by Barbara Grier & Christine
Cassidy. 272 pp. Love stories by Naiad Press authors.
          ISBN 1-56280-086-8   14.95

MISS PETTIBONE AND MISS McGRAW by Brenda Weathers.
208 pp. A charming ghostly love story.   ISBN 1-56280-151-1   10.95

CHANGES by Jackie Calhoun. 208 pp. Involved romance and
relationships.   ISBN 1-56280-083-3   10.95

FAIR PLAY by Rose Beecham. 256 pp. 3rd Amanda Valentine
Mystery.   ISBN 1-56280-081-7   10.95

PAYBACK by Celia Cohen. 176 pp. A gripping thriller of romance,
revenge and betrayal.   ISBN 1-56280-084-1   10.95

THE BEACH AFFAIR by Barbara Johnson. 224 pp. Sizzling
summer romance/mystery/intrigue.   ISBN 1-56280-090-6   10.95

GETTING THERE by Robbi Sommers. 192 pp. Nobody does it
like Robbi!   ISBN 1-56280-099-X   10.95

FINAL CUT by Lisa Haddock. 208 pp. 2nd Carmen Ramirez
Mystery.   ISBN 1-56280-088-4   10.95

FLASHPOINT by Katherine V. Forrest. 256 pp. A Lesbian
blockbuster!   ISBN 1-56280-079-5   11.95

CLAIRE OF THE MOON by Nicole Conn. Audio Book —Read
by Marianne Hyatt.   ISBN 1-56280-113-9   16.95

FOR LOVE AND FOR LIFE: INTIMATE PORTRAITS OF
LESBIAN COUPLES by Susan Johnson. 224 pp.
          ISBN 1-56280-091-4   14.95

DEVOTION by Mindy Kaplan. 192 pp. See the movie — read
the book!   ISBN 1-56280-093-0   10.95

SOMEONE TO WATCH by Jaye Maiman. 272 pp. 4th Robin
Miller Mystery.   ISBN 1-56280-095-7   10.95

GREENER THAN GRASS by Jennifer Fulton. 208 pp. A young
woman — a stranger in her bed.   ISBN 1-56280-092-2   10.95

TRAVELS WITH DIANA HUNTER by Regine Sands. Erotic
lesbian romp. Audio Book (2 cassettes)   ISBN 1-56280-107-4   16.95

CABIN FEVER by Carol Schmidt. 256 pp. Sizzling suspense
and passion. ISBN 1-56280-089-1 10.95

THERE WILL BE NO GOODBYES by Laura DeHart Young. 192
pp. Romantic love, strength, and friendship. ISBN 1-56280-103-1 10.95

FAULTLINE by Sheila Ortiz Taylor. 144 pp. Joyous comic
lesbian novel. ISBN 1-56280-108-2 9.95

OPEN HOUSE by Pat Welch. 176 pp. 4th Helen Black Mystery.
ISBN 1-56280-102-3 10.95

ONCE MORE WITH FEELING by Peggy J. Herring. 240 pp.
Lighthearted, loving romantic adventure. ISBN 1-56280-089-2 11.95

FOREVER by Evelyn Kennedy. 224 pp. Passionate romance — love
overcoming all obstacles. ISBN 1-56280-094-9 10.95

WHISPERS by Kris Bruyer. 176 pp. Romantic ghost story
ISBN 1-56280-082-5 10.95

NIGHT SONGS by Penny Mickelbury. 224 pp. 2nd Gianna Maglione
Mystery. ISBN 1-56280-097-3 10.95

GETTING TO THE POINT by Teresa Stores. 256 pp. Classic
southern Lesbian novel. ISBN 1-56280-100-7 10.95

PAINTED MOON by Karin Kallmaker. 224 pp. Delicious
Kallmaker romance. ISBN 1-56280-075-2 11.95

THE MYSTERIOUS NAIAD edited by Katherine V. Forrest &
Barbara Grier. 320 pp. Love stories by Naiad Press authors.
ISBN 1-56280-074-4 14.95

DAUGHTERS OF A CORAL DAWN by Katherine V. Forrest.
240 pp. Tenth Anniversay Edition. ISBN 1-56280-104-X 11.95

BODY GUARD by Claire McNab. 208 pp. 6th Carol Ashton
Mystery. ISBN 1-56280-073-6 11.95

CACTUS LOVE by Lee Lynch. 192 pp. Stories by the beloved
storyteller. ISBN 1-56280-071-X 9.95

SECOND GUESS by Rose Beecham. 216 pp. 2nd Amanda Valentine
Mystery. ISBN 1-56280-069-8 9.95

A RAGE OF MAIDENS by Lauren Wright Douglas. 240 pp. 6th Caitlin
Reece Mystery. ISBN 1-56280-068-X 10.95

TRIPLE EXPOSURE by Jackie Calhoun. 224 pp. Romantic drama
involving many characters. ISBN 1-56280-067-1 10.95

UP, UP AND AWAY by Catherine Ennis. 192 pp. Delightful
romance. ISBN 1-56280-065-5 11.95

PERSONAL ADS by Robbi Sommers. 176 pp. Sizzling short
stories. ISBN 1-56280-059-0 11.95

CROSSWORDS by Penny Sumner. 256 pp. 2nd Victoria Cross
Mystery. ISBN 1-56280-064-7 9.95

SWEET CHERRY WINE by Carol Schmidt. 224 pp. A novel of
suspense.   ISBN 1-56280-063-9   9.95
CERTAIN SMILES by Dorothy Tell. 160 pp. Erotic short stories.
                                                ISBN 1-56280-066-3   9.95
EDITED OUT by Lisa Haddock. 224 pp. 1st Carmen Ramirez
Mystery.   ISBN 1-56280-077-9   9.95
WEDNESDAY NIGHTS by Camarin Grae. 288 pp. Sexy
adventure.   ISBN 1-56280-060-4   10.95
SMOKEY O by Celia Cohen. 176 pp. Relationships on the
playing field.   ISBN 1-56280-057-4   9.95
KATHLEEN O'DONALD by Penny Hayes. 256 pp. Rose and
Kathleen find each other and employment in 1909 NYC.
                                                ISBN 1-56280-070-1   9.95
STAYING HOME by Elisabeth Nonas. 256 pp. Molly and Alix
want a baby . . . or do they?   ISBN 1-56280-076-0   10.95
TRUE LOVE by Jennifer Fulton. 240 pp. Six lesbians searching
for love in all the "right" places.   ISBN 1-56280-035-3   10.95
KEEPING SECRETS by Penny Mickelbury. 208 pp. 1st Gianna
Maglione Mystery.   ISBN 1-56280-052-3   9.95
THE ROMANTIC NAIAD edited by Katherine V. Forrest &
Barbara Grier. 336 pp. Love stories by Naiad Press authors.
                                                ISBN 1-56280-054-X   14.95
UNDER MY SKIN by Jaye Maiman. 336 pp. 3rd Robin Miller
Mystery.   ISBN 1-56280-049-3.   10.95
CAR POOL by Karin Kallmaker. 272pp. Lesbians on wheels
and then some!   ISBN 1-56280-048-5   10.95
NOT TELLING MOTHER: STORIES FROM A LIFE by Diane
Salvatore. 176 pp. Her 3rd novel.   ISBN 1-56280-044-2   9.95
GOBLIN MARKET by Lauren Wright Douglas. 240pp. 5th Caitlin
Reece Mystery.   ISBN 1-56280-047-7   10.95
LONG GOODBYES by Nikki Baker. 256 pp. 3rd Virginia Kelly
Mystery.   ISBN 1-56280-042-6   9.95
FRIENDS AND LOVERS by Jackie Calhoun. 224 pp. Mid-
western Lesbian lives and loves.   ISBN 1-56280-041-8   11.95
THE CAT CAME BACK by Hilary Mullins. 208 pp. Highly
praised Lesbian novel.   ISBN 1-56280-040-X   9.95

These are just a few of the many Naiad Press titles — we are the oldest and
largest lesbian/feminist publishing company in the world. We also offer an
enormous selection of lesbian video products. Please request a complete
catalog. We offer personal service; we encourage and welcome direct mail
orders from individuals who have limited access to bookstores carrying our
publications.